LEX

KAT T. MASEN

Kat T. Masen

LEX

A Dark Love Series Companion Novella
Dark Love Series Short Stories

Copyright 2022 Kat T. Masen
All Rights Reserved

ISBN: 979-8887969657
979-8846017078

Editing by More Than Words Copyediting and Proofreading
Proofing by Nicki at Swish Design & Editing
Cover design by The Book Cover Boutique
Cover Image Copyright 2022
First Edition 2022
All Rights Reserved

NOTE TO READERS

This companion novella is a collection of memories from Lex Edwards' POV from the *Dark Love* and *Forbidden Love* series.

To truly enjoy this book, it's recommended it be read after the completion of both series.

While there are many moments that didn't make it to this book, I hope you enjoy the trip down memory lane.

And don't you worry your little reader heart out. No story will be left unfinished. Every character will get a turn sharing their memories.

Even *Eric*...

ONE

Present

"**A**re you sure you can handle this, Dad?"

Amelia wrinkles her brows, waiting for me to reassure her since it's five days she'll be away from her children. If my memory serves correct, Charlotte was a mess the first time we left the girls for the same period of time. Several times on the drive to the airport, she asked if we could turn back because she didn't think Ava would sleep at night. Also, she worried Amelia might have accidentally burned my parents' house down.

"We've gone over this," Will intervenes in a calming tone even though he's trying to multi-task and type on his phone. "You'll be too drunk on cocktails to even remember having children."

A heavy sigh escapes Amelia as she narrows her eyes at Will.

"You're not helping me calm down."

"Amelia, how many times have we discussed this? You need to meet with a client. I need to meet with some clients," he reminds her tactfully. "It's business mixed with some pleasure. You won't have time to worry about the kids because before you know it, you'll be back on a flight to LA and dealing with a son who thinks Pennywise is real thanks to some idiot at preschool, and one who has a sudden fascination for using your lipstick all over our walls like he's Picasso."

I'm half-expecting Amelia to argue back since she is very much like Charlotte and must have the last word. As for Will, much like myself, you pick your battles. Women, specifically Charlotte and Amelia, are stubborn and refuse to back down just to prove a point.

Charlotte walks into the kitchen with one grandchild in her arms and another following behind her. Her chocolate brown hair falls perfectly to her collarbone, only to be tugged by Ava's daughter, River.

She moves around the kitchen so effortlessly, unaffected by the baby touching her hair or our grandson, Archer, pleading for a cookie before bedtime.

Even though years have passed, if possible, Charlotte is more beautiful than when I made her my wife. Watching her with our grandchildren is just how I envisioned our life would be once our kids grew. But, of course, this is after I accepted my daughters would not join a nunnery and stay celibate.

"Millie, relax. You don't see me all in fretful mother mode," Ava says with a wide grin, unusually relaxed, given she's known to panic at times.

Beside her, Austin shakes his head with a knowing smirk while taking River from Charlotte so Archer can get the attention he demands from his grandmother. Charlotte crouches to Archer's level, talking to him quietly to which he nods with an endearing smile. Bets are Charlotte has negotiated one cookie, but he must eat all his dinner. Even with the kids, she knows how to negotiate so we don't end up with kids running around on a sugar high.

"Perhaps, this is from the shots of tequila you drank before we came here to stop yourself from crying," Austin casually mentions.

"I had something in my eye," Ava drags, glancing in the opposite direction to Austin.

"Oh?" He muses, raising his eyes with delight. "Because it didn't seem to bother you during your retelling of the time your mom left you for Adriana's birthday in Cancun, then you cried so hard you puked on the living room floor."

Charlotte shakes her head with a groan. "If ever I had mom guilt, that was the moment."

"Sorry, Mom." Ava chuckles softly, then moves closer to River to caress her cheek. "I know my babies are in the best hands this week."

"Amelia, Ava," I say gently. "It will be fine. We've had all the kids overnight. What are a few more days? Enjoy your trip with Addison and Masen."

Ava's eldest daughter, Emmy, climbs into my lap, abandoning her boy cousins, who are now yelling in the living room. Emmy curls up into my chest, placing her thumb in her mouth while playing with the buttons of my shirt.

"Look at the old fella," Will goads with a broad smile. "He'll be fine. He has everything ready for tomorrow's big presentation and will sleep like a baby tonight."

Charlotte shakes her head with annoyance since I promised to help and not be distracted by work. That was before I found out a sought-after hotel chain was going on the market in Singapore because of an upcoming divorce proceeding.

"Speaking of this presentation, where are your numbers?" I question Will.

"Sitting in your inbox," he informs smugly. "Drop the ball already? Might need to send you to the old folks' home."

Not many people in my life can get away with this talk, but Will Romano is damn lucky he's my son-in-law and a brilliant man in the boardroom. Even before his relationship with Amelia, I knew this kid had talent. He's an innovator, a dying breed since many are quick to label themselves this but fall short in the act.

"Nice dig, kid. Don't call me in the old folks' home when you need me to sign off on a deal because you can't read Cantonese. I'll be busy playing bingo with my wife."

Ava claps her hands. "Okay, you two, enough smack talk. We need to go, or we'll miss our flight."

"Um, aren't you forgetting about the other happy couple?" Amelia reminds Ava.

"They're probably having sex... " Ava blurts out, " ... since Masen flew back from San Antonio a few hours ago."

I bow my head, clenching my teeth, trying to remind myself of my girls being adults now. Yet, no matter how hard I try, the state of unrest is engrained into me. My chest tightens as Charlotte pats my shoulder with a soft laugh.

"Oh shit, sorry Dad," Ava mumbles only to continue, "... but true story."

The door opens, saving me from a stroke. What perfect timing since it's Masen and Addison joining us. I bury Ava's inappropriate references to focus on them with a welcoming smile. It's only been a few months since they moved to San Francisco, but I miss seeing Addison since she's no longer a short drive away.

"Hey, everyone," they greet in unison.

Around the room, Masen and Addison hug everyone until they reach where I'm sitting, prompting me to stand from the chair.

Placing Emmy down, I stand tall, admiring how grown-up and mature Addison has become. Of all the girls, she's been the easiest, and perhaps it's because she's lived a simple life without unnecessary drama. The relationship with Masen is not something I'm against since I've known the kid since he was born. I'm just hoping they take the time to focus on their careers before starting a family. Masen has already taken over the CEO position at Lantern Publishing, and Addison just started a new job while finishing her degree at the same time.

Addison wraps her arms around my waist, laying her face against my chest as I kiss the top of her head. Inside my arms, she's still my little girl.

"I've missed you, kid."

"I know. I've missed you too," she murmurs, pulling away slowly. "I'm still waiting for you to come visit. You'd love the view from our apartment. It's very Lex Edwards."

I chuckle softly. "And exactly what does that mean?"

"A view of the Bay Bridge located in the heart of the historic Financial District."

Unable to hold back my smile, I caress her cheek with the back of my hand. "You know me better than I know myself. Once you return, I'm sure your mother and I can make some time to visit."

Ava calls attention to the time, prompting everyone to say their goodbyes and leave for the airport.

As suspected, Amelia cries while hugging her boys. They hug her tight, asking her if she has happy tears, to which she nods with a smile. Her youngest son, Alexander, named after me, of course, is only four months old and too young to understand what is happening.

Ava, who previously was relaxed, suddenly appears anxious. Austin is quick to notice, rubbing her lower back as her face turns white like she's about to be sick. He asks her if she needs to use the bathroom, but she shakes her head and straightens her shoulders. They both kiss their daughters, then each one of them says goodbye to Charlotte and me.

"Are you sure you can handle this, Dad?" Amelia asks again.

"Yes, Amelia."

Will scratches his chin. "Don't let me down in tomorrow's presentation. I might accidentally ask the Chairman in Cantonese if he enjoys his wife in the hotel again."

"Oh my god, you asked that?" Amelia cringes.

"I was meant to ask if he and his wife enjoyed spending time using the hotel's facilities. As Lex said, Cantonese is not my strongest skill."

"No, it isn't," I agree, then continue, "... let me lead tomorrow. You will know your cues."

"Are we ready?" Masen asks, checking the time. "The traffic on the 405 is a nightmare at this time."

"The 405 is a nightmare all the time," Addison corrects him.

"Your father and I will be fine, I promise," Charlotte reassures them. "Now, have fun, enjoy your child-free time, and we'll FaceTime once you're settled, okay?"

Masen opens the door, prompting everyone to follow him. Since he doesn't have kids, his patience wears thin waiting for everyone to say their goodbyes. The drivers are outside, waiting to load their suitcases since they need two cars to get to the airport.

With Charlotte beside me, we wave goodbye to the kids, but just before Ava climbs in, she stops with her hand resting on the door.

"No sex with Mom while the kids are awake. Control yourself, Dad."

And just like that, Ava knows exactly how to make a moment memorable. Beside me, Charlotte laughs, knocking into my side with her elbow. "Did you hear that? We have rules."

The door closes, then the driver toots his horn as they drive down the driveway.

I nod with a smirk, turning to face Charlotte as I stare into her beautiful brown eyes. No words need to pass between us because everything we have, everything we are, can be felt with just one weighted gaze.

But then I remember the rules.

I don't obey rules, not when it interferes with me devouring my wife's body. My thumb grazes her bottom lip as she releases a sigh.

"And rules were made to broken, sweetheart."

TWO

Present

The younger children finally fall asleep after what can only be described as a hectic night.

Thankfully, none of them cried for their parents. Instead, it was quite the opposite. They were excited to be sleeping over, and energy levels took a while to dwindle until we managed to bathe them and read multiple stories, waiting until gentle snores graced the room.

I'd forgotten just how exhausting children can be, but I make a mental note to keep it to myself and not show Charlotte my weakness.

"Okay, kids are exhausting." She lets out a long-winded breath, closing her eyes momentarily. "How did we raise four girls?"

My lips curve upward into a smile. "You are supermom, that's how."

"C'mon, I couldn't have done it without you. Addy's soccer games? How you had the patience for that is beyond me."

"I gladly took Addy's soccer games over Ava's ballet lessons."

Charlotte snorts. "All fun and games until they hit puberty, and those activities were no longer fun. I can't recall the last time I've seen Ava perform a pirouette."

We walk a few steps to the room Ashton is sleeping in. Amelia recommended separating the boys for our own sanity. Apparently, if they're sleeping in the same room, you're guaranteed one will wake the other one up at some god-awful hour then a fight will break out due to exhaustion.

My hand rests on the doorknob as I knock with the other gently.

"Hey, buddy, still awake?"

Ashton turns to his side, resting his face in his hands. "I'm just thinking."

I glance at Charlotte, wondering what a five-year-old thinks about that doesn't involve monster trucks or dinosaurs. Amelia mentioned his Pokémon obsession, something I was forced to learn when Will was a young boy and went through the same stage.

We both sit beside Ashton, careful not to squash him.

"Thinking is sometimes nice to do alone," Charlotte assures him.

Ashton purses his lips with his wide blue eyes staring back at us. It's not unusual for Ashton to stay the night, so we decorated this room just for him. He chose the colors and theme. It's nice to see other colors used besides pink.

"Did you know I have another Mommy who lives in heaven?"

My eyes fixate on him, careful not to swing to Charlotte like a desperate man calling for a life jacket. The voices in my head are running rampant, unsure how to respond to such a loaded question. Yet, my smile remains fixed, praying Charlotte is the first to respond.

"Yes," she simply says with a smile. "You're a very lucky boy to have two mommies."

Ashton's expression remains blank, not giving us any indication of how he is feeling about this.

"Daddy and Mommy said I was so special, they had to take me home because they were so sad without me."

I nod, the only response I'm able to make. "Yes, it's true."

Charlotte moves the loose strand of hair away from his forehead.

"There are so many ways to be part of a family," she tells him softly. "And I thank God every day he chose you to be part of our family."

"But if God chose me to be part of this family, why can't my other mommy stay too?"

The walls inside my chest begin to cave, the breathing becoming tighter and restrictive. How do you even explain to him the car accident that killed his biological mother? Or even the fact of his biological father not wanting to keep him? Oddly so, I've crossed paths with Stewart Knight and have a very low opinion of him. He knows Ashton is my grandson, though at least he's smart enough to avoid me when we see each other.

I lean forward, staring into Ashton's eyes while cupping his hand in mine. His hand is so small, and a part of me often wonders if this is what it would have felt like if our son had survived.

"Your other mommy was so special that God had plans for her. Sometimes, this happens," I say softly. "But you know what? You are our first grandchild, and that's just the way it was always meant to be."

Ashton lets out a small yawn, then, briefly, a small smile on his tired face.

"I like being the first. Maybe I'm special too."

Slowly, I lean in to kiss his forehead. "You're very special. Now, it's bedtime, kiddo."

Ashton nods, then quickly tugs my sleeve. "Don't forget we're going to the park tomorrow for my soccer game."

A small laugh leaves my lips. "You're talking to an ex-soccer coach. I promise I will be here after work to take you and your brother."

"I love you, Grandpapa."

"Love you too, kiddo."

Charlotte tucks him in before gently bringing the door to a close as I wait just outside the room. The welcoming silence is the sound of heaven until her hand reaches out for my own. With a heaviness upon us, we walk quietly to our master bedroom, which is only a few doors down.

Inside the room, we prepare for bed in silence, unsure how to navigate our thoughts from an innocent moment that came from our grandson. After a quick shower, brushing my teeth, and changing into my bed shorts, I climb into bed, staring at my wedding ring while waiting for Charlotte to return.

My phone beeps on the nightstand beside m. It's nothing unusual, most likely work which for now can be ignored. There are other things on my mind and maybe other things I need to get off my chest.

Charlotte walks back into the bedroom dressed in her silk white pajamas' and then climbs into bed. Immediately, the fresh scent of soap engulfs the air between us.

"I have to admit, Ashton caught me off guard tonight," I say quietly, unsure how to articulate my thoughts.

"Well, I guess it was bound to come up. I know Will

and Amelia have always wanted to be open with Ashton."
Charlotte's chest rises, then falls with a sigh escaping her.
"They want him to know where he came from. I've seen this
a lot, of course. It's one of those things which you've just got
to somehow navigate through as a family."

"I understand, but don't you think he's too young?"

"Yes, no," Charlotte murmurs while toying with the
edge of the bedsheet. "There's never a right answer, nor is
there a predicted outcome. Some children ask questions out
of curiosity, and nothing changes in their lives. Then others
ask the questions, and it changes everything."

When it comes to family matters such as this, Charlotte
is the expert. Over her career, she's handled many family
law cases. Some, with a positive outcome, and others, where
she came home defeated because some deadbeat dad was
awarded custody of his children.

Charlotte continues, "Some parents choose to hide the
fact that their child is adopted or fostered, and you know, all
of these things really shouldn't matter if you have the love of
a parent and a family. But... I've never been in either situation myself, so maybe I would feel differently being on
either end."

My hand moves on top of hers, caressing it gently.
We've been blessed with our family, which I'm grateful for
daily. As for Will and Amelia, Ashton was always meant to
be in their lives. They made a big decision, one our whole
family is eternally grateful for.

"I can't imagine our lives without him," I say honestly.

"I think it's a positive thing Ashton is asking these questions early, but it's hard. He's our grandson. I don't want to
say the wrong things and upset Will and Amelia."

"He is our grandson," I repeat. "Maybe that's why this
feels harder."

Charlotte turns to face me, sensing my vulnerability. "Is there something you're afraid of? We won't lose him. I promise you Stewart has no parental rights to take his son back."

"If I'm being honest here, resentment maybe when he's older."

"You know that will never happen. Will and Amelia are amazing parents. Ashton is blessed to have them as they are blessed to have him. He has a supportive family, plus he has brothers and cousins, aunts and uncles. To add, he has us."

I let out a soft chuckle. "You forgot about Rocky and Nikki."

A sly smile plays on Charlotte's lips. "The jury is still out if Rocky's a good influence on Ashton."

"Will turned out pretty good," I remind her.

"Will turned out good because he went against everything Rocky taught him. I don't know where Will would've ended up if it weren't for Nikki. Probably managing some strip joint in a seedy part of Manhattan."

I'm damn proud of Will, especially since he dealt with me during those years he and Amelia were apart. In hindsight, I should have stayed out of their relationship. I'm guilty of making his life hell and being the reason why he was miserable for four years. He's proven to be the man for my daughter. In the end, that's all that matters now.

"You're right. Will goes against everything Rocky says, and he's a billionaire in his own right."

"Ashton is our grandson just as much as all the other children. Ultimately, it is Will and Amelia's responsibility to help him navigate through this. We are his grandparents, and I want to be there for them if they need us. It's new territory for us too."

"I know," I agree softly. "I just never expected to be this

involved with grandkids. I guess, I felt for the longest time, we raised our kids. Our job was done."

Charlotte pats my hand. "Speaking of raising children, I guess you forgot about one daughter who hasn't come back home yet. It's past her curfew."

All of a sudden, I remember Alexa. The occurrence with Ashton distracted me from the ongoing issue of my youngest daughter. I glance at the time. It's past ten on a school night. There is no text message from her to tell us she's running late or even just a courtesy text to tell us she's still alive wherever she is.

I take a deep breath trying to control my anger. No matter what I do with this kid, she refuses to fucking listen. Given her older sisters have moved out, she thinks she has the freedom to do whatever she pleases, and act like them. Yet, Alexa is forgetting she lives under our roof, and as far as I'm concerned, our rules.

"Charlotte," I voice in a stern tone. "I'm done with Alexa and this behavior. If it comes down to us taking her things off her, phone or car, I'm willing to do that. I'm serious. She's not a responsible adult yet. Alexa's in her senior year. She hasn't even applied for colleges."

"Lex, we've gone over this. College is Alexa's decision."

My blood begins to boil, my temper bubbling beneath the surface, ready to argue again over this broken record of an issue. "This isn't just Alexa's decision. She must attend college, and we have yet to have this proper discussion with her. Time is running out. If she expects me to pull strings to get her into a college, she will be incredibly disappointed. She will attend college just like her sisters."

"You have to stop comparing her to Millie, Ava, and Addy. They're different. Millie always wanted to go to law school and worked hard to make sure she got into Yale.

As for Ava, yeah, sure, she was a bit of a struggle. She wanted to go to college for the social aspect and parties, but regardless, she went and still graduated in business school." Charlotte takes a deep breath, knowing this is a very touchy subject with me. "Addy is much like Amelia, very academic. She sets goals and does everything in her power to achieve them."

All of what Charlotte is saying is true. Each one of our daughters has successfully navigated their way to adulthood. Yet if the truth is told, my faith in Alexa following their footsteps is disappearing by the minute. She's not afraid of Charlotte or me—disregarding our rules with no care for consequences. Of late, if the older girls join us for a family dinner, Alexa makes it out like she's held against her will, and spending time with us is a chore, not a privilege.

"We need to be easy on Alexa, okay? It's hard to be following the footsteps of three sisters who are very successful in their own right. So, perhaps when you are calmer and not angry that it's past her curfew, we can have a discussion about the future."

I cross my arms beneath my chest. "You expect me to sit here and do nothing?"

Charlotte leans over and grabs her phone from the nightstand. "I will text her and make sure she gets home within the next hour. Tomorrow, I will deal with her. As for you, please just give yourself a moment to remember Alexa is only eighteen."

"Exactly, Charlotte. She's only eighteen. She lives under our roof, under our rules. Do you remember what you were doing at eighteen?"

Beside me, Charlotte tilts her head with annoyance. "Sure, I was sleeping with my best friend's married older brother."

"Why are you getting annoyed with me? I'm pointing out the facts."

"I'm not arguing about this anymore, Lex. Tonight's been a little bit more than what we bargained for. You've got your presentation to focus on for tomorrow. I'm going to take the kids out for playtime in the park, then head over to Adriana's." Charlotte yawns, then continues, "I'll make sure Alexa is here for dinner tomorrow night. How does that sound?"

"It sounds like you're my bossy wife who probably needs to get laid."

"And it sounds like you're my controlling husband who has forgotten that we have a house full of grandkids."

"Are you saying we're supposed to be celibate for five days? I never signed up for this when I agreed for all of them to stay over," I remind her.

"I'm saying you're going to be exhausted, and sex will be the very last thing on your mind."

The thought of not touching Charlotte for five days is making me hard. Fuck, perhaps I'll wake her up at night once we know all the kids are fast asleep.

"Charlotte, baby, when it comes to you, sex is always the first thing on my mind."

Charlotte punches my arm with a soft laugh. "That's so romantic of you. Now go to sleep. I love you."

I let out a low-rumbling growl realizing tonight is not the night, especially since Alexa's absence weighs heavily on my mind.

"I'm going to head downstairs and wait for Alexa." I throw the sheets off me, grabbing my navy robe hanging near the bed.

"Fine," Charlotte groans. "I'll take my clothes off if that's what it's going to take for you to stay in bed."

I contemplate the offer, but my head is filled with anger and concern over our daughter's well-being.

"Go to sleep. I won't be long." I lean over and kiss Charlotte on the cheek.

Quietly, I head downstairs to wait for Alexa, careful not to wake any of the grandkids. According to Ava, River is a light sleeper. Since she's still an infant, the last thing I need is for a screaming baby to wake up, which in turn, can wake everyone.

The back door opens as soon as I turn the kitchen light on.

Alexa walks in, surprised to see me. My eyes are drawn to the short yellow dress she is wearing. Too short and too tight for a young girl. The anger inside me begins to swirl, forcing me to clench my fists to control myself. The girls all followed the dress code when they were growing up, though there were times Ava pushed to see how far she could get away with it.

"Oh," is all she says, avoiding eye contact with me.

"Oh?" I repeat in a cold tone. "Is that the only response I'll get from you, considering it's two hours past your curfew, and it's a school night?"

Alexa continues to ignore me, flicking her long chestnut brown hair over her shoulder as if I'm overreacting. Beneath her chest, she crosses her arms impatiently, waiting for me to call defeat and send her to her room.

"Anything you'd like to say, Alexandra?"

This time, she rolls her eyes with a puff of air leaving her lips.

"Let me guess. You're calling me Alexandra, so I'm in big trouble? Assuming I'm grounded, you'll take all my privileges from me because you are the controlling Lex Edwards."

The heat inside my body rises to boiling point. How dare she disrespect me like she's done nothing wrong. Charlotte's voice plays in my head, but as far as I'm concerned, no matter what I say or do, Alexa will go against me regardless.

"You're damn right you're grounded," I shout, slamming my fist on the counter. "How dare you worry your mother and me over your careless actions. You live in this house. You abide by our rules."

"I'm over your rules!" she yells back, eyes blazing with fire. "I didn't ask to be Lex Edwards' daughter. This life was thrust upon me."

"This life?" I tilt my head in confusion. "A life of having a roof over your head, food on the table, private schooling? I'm sorry. Please explain how awful it is for you to have what many children have to fight for."

"You have no idea." She lowers her head.

"No idea how spoiled you are? You have everything you want. Please, enlighten me. How terrible it is to grow up as our daughter?"

Slowly, her emerald eyes, the same shade as mine, lift to meet mine. There's something unexplainable in the weight of her stare, and for just a moment, I want to reassure her we love her despite this argument.

But my compassion is short-lived.

"I hate you."

And with her final words said, she storms out of the room, leaving me reeling. Never, in my time as a parent, have any of my girls ever used such strong language, even at the peak of our arguments.

Yet, the word hate is raw and soul-destroying, especially when your youngest daughter uses it so coldly.

It doesn't take long for Charlotte to come downstairs.

Alexa's stomping up the stairs would have been enough to wake Charlotte if she was sleeping.

The moment she walks into the kitchen, she crosses her arms with a judgmental expression, one I've seen many times.

"Lex, I told you we needed to deal with this in a different way. All you're doing is pushing her away. The more you push, the less control you have over her."

My lips pinch together, barely able to keep them shut in order not to lash out at Charlotte for Alexa's behavior. I chose to keep the conversation to myself because if Charlotte knew what Alexa said, it would upset her immensely.

When it came to business, I controlled everything.

But with Alexa, I've lost control. Charlotte is right, I've pushed, and Alexa is running as far away from me as possible.

Just as I'm about to tell Charlotte precisely what we're going to do with Alexa, a message appears on my screen. I half glance over, but then my eyes focus, slowly reading each word with a tightness forming in my chest.

My body freezes as I continue to read the message over and over again.

"Lex," Charlotte calls softly. "You've turned white. What's wrong?"

A coldness expands in my core, leaving me numb and without the ability to answer Charlotte. Then, I clear my throat, still staring at the text in disbelief.

"He's dead."

THREE

Present

The walls in my chest press against my lungs, making the simple act of breathing almost impossible.

Charlottes' wide eyes panic at my silence, but as always, she gives me a moment to collect myself without pushing me into deeper shock.

"BJ," I barely manage, my eyes falling to the floor. "Bentley James Woods."

The sound of Charlotte's heavy sigh echoes in the kitchen. Death itself, is never right with its timing, always shocking us no matter who the person may be.

"What happened?"

"Heart attack," I barely choke. "He passed away this morning."

I reread the text message but this time out loud. It was sent from a former employee of mine who is quite close to Bentley back in London.

"Lex," Charlotte's voice softens as she places her hand on my arm. "He was so young."

The reality is brutal with its force. It shines a light on my own mortality. Deep down, I know why this pain feels real, why it's hitting hard at this moment.

I lower my head. "He was my age."

Charlotte immediately shakes her head. "No, don't do this."

"If it can happen to a man like him, why can't it happen to a man like me?"

Suddenly, Charlotte grabs the front of my robe and pulls me into her. She buries her head into my chest while soft sobs escape her.

Death is not something we are strangers to. There have been loved ones from Charlotte's mother to my own father.

And the one which rocked us the most—Elijah.

My arms wrap around Charlotte to comfort her and ease the worry I know she is feeling. Seconds, maybe even minutes, pass of just silence. Then, slowly, she pulls away, but I keep her close.

"When was the last time you spoke to him?"

I shrug, trying to do the math in my head, but it's all a blur. Our entrance into the business world is what brought us into each other's lives and the only thing we had in common. At least, the only thing I *choose* to remember we had in common.

"I'm not sure, maybe a year ago."

"Once we know when the funeral will take place, we must attend," Charlotte insists while taking a deep breath, but I half-listen. "I forgot we have all the grandkids. Surely, it will be at least a week to prepare everything. The kids will be back by then, and we can go straight to London. Adriana can stay here to watch over Alexa. Maybe we should ask his family if they need help with anything?"

"He didn't have a family. An only child and his parents are long gone," I inform her, shedding light on the facts. "Never married because he enjoyed the freedom to sleep around."

"I can't imagine how sad that must be to not have family and to live life without someone you love ..." Charlotte trails off.

I force a small smile, then bring her hand to my lips and place a gentle kiss.

"Let's not imagine it," I remind her softly. "We have everything we ever wanted."

Our bags were packed within four hours of the kids returning from Cancun. Then, we hopped straight into a private plane to Heathrow.

All week, I tried my best to focus on our grandkids. They proved to be the best distraction with all their demands and need for our attention. Though, when their parents arrived, I breathed a sigh of relief. I love them all, but silence is golden. Also, enjoying a meal without inter-ruption is a blessing no one speaks of.

As for Alexa, she avoided me since our argument. She had no words, and I had no words. What do you say when your daughter says she hates you? The wound is still open, but thankfully, she did listen and was home every night. With Adriana watching her, I made sure to inform my sister of Alexa's rules. Adriana is much more relaxed with her own children, but I also know I can rely on her when needed.

Ten and a half hours later, the plane's wheels hit the tarmac at Heathrow. The landing is reasonably smooth, and in typical England style, the sky is gray with the sun missing behind a cluster of clouds.

Visiting London is not something we often do, but of the times I've been back, the nostalgia is a force to be reckoned with. Every place, every street we drove down, has some memory attached to it. Some are pleasant, and some I would rather forget.

We chose to stay at The Four Seasons at Park Lane as our properties are all tenanted. Unlike Manhattan, it never made sense for us to purchase a place to stay since our visits were few and far between. The kids always preferred to spend time in France at our chateau because their cousins were next door when Noah and Kate's visited too.

Our flight arrived in the late afternoon, making it dinner time when we check-in. Charlotte appears exhausted, despite her resting on the plane. During the last week, she did her best to juggle taking care of the kids and trying to work when I took over. But, of course, Charlotte refused to slow down because she didn't want to fall behind despite having a competent team working in the office.

"Why don't I order room service? We have a big day tomorrow."

Charlotte simply nods, too tired to even form a sentence, falling limp on the plush sofa inside the sitting room. When the food arrives, she takes some bites but looks close to falling asleep at the table.

"I don't think I can make it." She yawns.

A soft chuckle escapes me. "I'm surprised you didn't fall asleep after the first bite. Go to sleep."

"Are you coming?"

I rub my chin with a smirk. "Is that a question?"

Charlotte lets out a huff but follows with a grin. "Are you coming to bed? Don't get offended if I fall asleep if you try anything."

"We've been married for what?"

"A long time," she answers with a knowing smile.

When it comes to Charlotte, I'm greedy and selfish about my needs. But, at this moment, I'm sympathetic to my wife's needs. It's been a very long week for both of us, and even I feel worn down and tired.

As the night falls, so does Charlotte into a deep sleep. I'm hoping to do the same but find myself tossing and turning with flashes of my past life with BJ. When it all becomes too much, I turn over and glance at the clock. It's just after midnight.

Inside my suitcase, there is a bottle of sleeping pills. It's rare for me to take medications, but given the nature of tomorrow, I hop out of bed and pop one, eventually falling asleep.

The following day, I manage to wake up despite the aided assistance of the pills. As I slide my arms inside the black suit jacket, Charlotte stands beside me in the mirror. Even for a funeral, she looks stunning in the simple black dress she wears.

"Are you okay?" she gently asks with concern.

"I'm fine," I simply answer. "We should leave in order to make the ceremony and the burial."

BJ was a man who wasn't fond of commitment. He often joked about my life, referring to Charlotte as the ball and chain. His British humor wasn't offensive nor belittling, and even though he called Charlotte such names, he equally enjoyed her company whenever we were together. She knew how to tame the bastard in her presence, and because of that—he respected her very much.

Perhaps, in hindsight, his humor was masking his loneliness.

Today, his life of solitude is noticeable.

Attending his funeral are only a small number of people. His former nanny, an elderly lady, is sitting in a wheelchair being assisted by a nurse. The woman's posture is fallen, her limbs frail and thin, yet inside her pale hands, she clutches onto rosary beads with her eyes closed.

Standing in a huddle are business partners he had dealt with of late. Accompanying them are their partners. I see one of my former employees, the one who sent me the text message.

Then, there is his polo club team. They wear their uniform to honor him—pale blue shirts with white pants. BJ was fond of the sport having grown up in England. Personally, I had no interest even though he tried numerous times to make me join and play while I lived in London.

But, notably absent is anyone in his life who meant more to him than an acquaintance.

Kate sent her condolences, though I never expected her to attend. Their relationship, if you could even call it that, was a long time ago. At the time, I chose to ignore what was going on because they were grown adults and their personal lives were theirs, provided it did not affect business.

However, typical Kate still organized a large wreath of flowers for today despite her ties with him being a thing of the past.

As we stand in the cemetery, a minister reads from the bible while we pay our respects and say goodbye. A man from the polo team says a prayer, but no one comes forward to give any personal tributes.

Perhaps, just like me, there are no words to be said.

During the ceremony, Charlotte holds my hand tight behind the oversized sunglasses she wears.

And just like that, it all ends.

Bentley James Woods is laid to rest.

A moment of silence is given before people begin to walk away to the cars parked beside the green lawns.

My feet are planted firmly in the spot I'm standing, staring quietly at the open ground which holds the body of a man who once was my saving grace.

His life walked a path similar to my own. BJ was forced to take control of a family empire, thrust upon the ruthless world of money. Just like me, he battled his demons, and this is what brought us together.

But with this came darkness.

A time when my demons were tormenting me over how I treated Charlotte and ended things between us. How the lies of my former wife, and my father's actions led me to lose the one person I promised never to leave behind.

How my own weakness damaged everything, we were beyond repair.

When days and nights were a blur, I consumed narcotics and anything I could get my hands on to take away the pain, including women. On many occasions, more than one at a time, and sometimes it was me and BJ with one woman.

A woman who demanded we tie her up and treat her like a slave for our own satisfaction. The vicious cycle we both found ourselves in was toxic and disturbing, but while high—nothing else mattered.

The tightness inside my chest restricts my ability to breathe at an average pace, but then, I admit what weighs so heavily on my mind.

"This could have been me."

Charlotte squeezes my hand tightly, silently shaking her head.

"It's not you. So, why would you say it could've been you?"

"Because Charlotte, once upon a time, this was me. I was alone," I clench my teeth with a bittersweet pain. "I did the same things he did. Things I'm not proud of. But then I ran into you in the restaurant, and it all changed."

"It's fate," she whispers beside me. "We both did things we weren't proud of, but fate led us to each other."

My eyes fixate on the ground as all my mistakes rise to the surface.

"Lex, everything you have is everything you deserve. You are worth all the blessings you've been given."

Releasing a breath, I nod, then smile, leaning over to kiss the top of Charlotte's head.

I am blessed.

I've been given a life filled with a family I never expected. Experienced love in every form, and above everything, a life partner I'm proud to call my wife.

Yet, the longer I stand here, the more I think about how easily my life could have taken a different turn. I could have been the one lying in this cold ground.

Bentley James Woods is who I would have become if I didn't make a last-minute decision to attend the meeting at the Japanese restaurant where I ran into Charlotte.

The irony of this all is BJ was the one who pushed me to meet with investors that day. He had heard some unsettling rumors of one of the stakeholders laundering money and insisted I make an appearance to show him who's boss.

And that's where it all began, again.

Gazing into the eyes of the woman who left her mark a long time ago, in the backyard of my parents' home, inside the treehouse, the memories begin to play, some sweet, some painful.

But all of them lead to us ...

FOUR

The time with the comic book

The knock on the door is all too familiar.

I take a deep breath, ignoring the sound while continuing to pack my bag. The music blaring from my speakers is loud enough to pretend I don't hear anything else. My gaze turns toward the clock to make a note of the time. If I'm late for my shift, my boss will kill me.

The creak of the door catches my attention despite the music, but I remain quiet while rolling my eyes with annoyance.

"Alex," Dad voices in a less-than-pleasing tone. "I'd like to have a word with you."

My back is still facing him because I know whatever he has to say is something I

don't want to hear. His feet move toward my bookshelf, where he turns the knob to reduce the volume to practically nothing.

"I'm going to be late for work," I inform him.

"This won't take long," he insists, purposely moving his

position so I'm forced to see him. "We just received your report card, and I'm rather disappointed."

I close my eyes, willing to disappear from his lectures on how I'm a screw-up. God forbid I don't live up to his ideal role of the doctor's son. What the fuck did he want from me? I'm fifteen. It's not the end of the world.

"These are not acceptable grades to get into college, and furthermore, to study medicine." Any minute now, he'll start lecturing on how it takes discipline to become a doctor. "It takes discipline, Alex. I know you're fifteen, but good habits are formed early. You've got a long road ahead of you, but the reward is greater than you can ever imagine."

I glance at the time again. Now I'm going to be extra late with no real excuse besides my father being an asshole.

"I need to go, or I'll lose my job."

"About the job." Dad clears his throat, then folds his arms, trying to show off his authority. "If working at the pizza place will affect your studies, then you need to consider cutting down your shifts."

"Cutting down my shifts?" I repeat, raising my voice. "I only work two shifts because of school and sports. I need money."

"Your education is more important than any frivolous purchase of yours."

My hand grips around the strap of my backpack as I try to control my temper. He won't give me money, expecting me to work hard for what I want. Yet, in the same breath, he wants me to quit my job to fulfill his dreams for me.

As I'm about to step out, Dad places his hand on my shoulder to stop me.

"This is not negotiable, Alex. Those grades better improve."

I shove my body away from his hand, running down the

hall and stairs. When I'm outside the house, I hop on my bike to peddle as fast as I can to work. The neon restaurant sign is just down the street and in my vision. It's a weekend, and the lunch shift is usually quick if I focus on what I need to do. The streets are lined with cars, and the day is sunny, bringing everyone to town.

I'm only four minutes late to work, but it's enough for my manager to yell at me and spend the next three hours treating me like shit. I fucking hate this job, busting my ass for a measly few dollars an hour plus tips if it's a good day.

The shift drags on, and so does my mood. The minute I clock off, I don't even say goodbye, packing my things and ignoring how I stink of grease. Finally, I'm ready to forget today's existence and go crash in my room.

Then, my eyes shift toward the comic bookstore across the street. I grab my bike but decide to push it across the road rather than ride it.

I'm pulled to the display at the front of the store. Inside the window is the new Batman comic. I stare at it in awe, remembering how I saw the exact same one in Sacramento a few weeks ago, but I was with Dad, and he said under no circumstances was I to waste my money on a comic book.

He can fuck right off with his rules. My hands push on the glass as the door chime sounds upon me entering. Eagerly, I move to the counter and request to see the comic book.

"Sorry, dude. No one touches it," the guy behind the counter, obnoxiously chewing gum, answers rudely.

"I've got money to buy it."

He raises his brows. "Oh yeah, prove it?"

I pull my wallet out, then remove the bills. Every single cent I've saved over the last few months.

"Hmm, okay."

He goes to the window and removes it carefully, then places it in front of me. The artwork and colors look to be in mint condition, and just because I can, I remove my cash from inside my wallet and place it on the counter.

"I'll take it."

The guy appears surprised, quickly taking my cash and storing it in the register. Next, he packages up the comic book in some special plastic, then slides it into a brown paper bag.

The comic book is nestled inside my jacket against my chest on the ride home. I'm riding incredibly slow in an effort not to damage anything. Thankfully, the sun is still out, so there's no chance of rain.

As soon as I get home, it's straight to the shower to wash off the grease. Of course, since it's a Saturday, I've nothing planned besides chilling and catching up on my schoolwork to avoid my father's wrath.

I throw on my gray sweats and favorite Laker's tee, then head to the kitchen to grab something to eat before sitting down to read my comic book. Inside the kitchen, an empty plate sits on the counter with a note beside it in Mom's handwriting:

Make sure you share these cookies.
Love Mom

All I see are crumbs on the white plate. With an annoyed huff, I storm into the living room to see Adriana sprawled on the couch watching some girly movie. Her hair is tied into a weird ponytail with colorful bows sticking out like a clown on crack.

"You're so annoying," I yell at her, even though she ignores me. "Mom said to share the cookies."

"You snooze. You lose."

"I was working, not sitting around looking like a circus freak."

Adriana is quick to sit up, crossing her arms in defiance.

"Shut up, or I'll tell Mom and Dad you were kissing that girl at the library when you were supposed to be studying."

My eyes widen as my blood begins to boil.

"How do you know that?"

Her lips curve up into a fake smile. "I was listening to your phone call."

I'm about to go over and strangle the little shit, but instead, I hear my parents' voices in my head from the last time I threw a book at her. Frankly, she deserved it for snooping in my room.

Having the world's most annoying little sister does nothing to relax me after my shift. I storm out of the room, stopping in our house's foyer, then head outside to our old treehouse where hopefully Adriana won't find me.

It's been a long time since I've climbed up the chipped wooden steps, but something draws me toward the place I enjoyed so much as a kid. Careful to balance my comic book in one hand without damaging it, I manage to climb to the top but hear a sobbing sound. My eyes dart to the corner where a young girl has buried her head into her arms with her knees raised. Her worn-out jeans have dirt all over them, yet I'm drawn to the chocolate-colored hair that flows so long it almost touches the floor.

My feet step on the wooden floor, making a creaking sound that catches her attention. Suddenly, her big brown eyes widen at my presence.

"I'm... I'm Charlotte," she stumbles, choking back her tears.

Unsure of what to do or say, I scratch the back of my neck. "You must be Adriana's friend."

She simply nods. There is a sadness about her. Not just the bloodshot eyes from the tears she's shedding, but the way she appears defeated as if the weight of the world is on her shoulders.

I'm not sure why I sit next to her, considering she's my sister's friend and Adriana is a pain in the ass.

"Do you want to talk?"

Charlotte continues to sit quietly though she nervously pulls at the thread of her ripped jeans. "My parents had a big fight. They fight every day." She drops her eyes with a quivering voice. "My mom says my dad is the biggest mistake of her life. Then she left."

"I'm sorry. I'm sure she doesn't mean it."

"It's not the first time she's left, but it's been three days." Charlotte turns to face me with wide eyes. "Do you think I should look for her?"

What did I know about adult problems? My parents are happily married and rarely fight. Surprisingly, Dad is super nice to Mom all the time. He even treats Adriana like a princess. I'm the one he likes to pick on. But this isn't about me. Something about Charlotte's sadness stirs something unknown inside me. Almost like I need to protect her.

"It will work out. Whatever is meant to be will be. This isn't your fault, okay?"

Charlotte's lips begin to tremble, and even when I try to ignore how sad this little girl is right now over what appears to be a selfish mother, I can't seem to walk away and leave her alone.

I'm not sure why I pull my comic book out of the brown paper bag, but I do so to avoid any further conversations about her family.

She tilts her head while sniffing, then draws her brows upon noticing the comic book.

"I love Batman." Charlotte smiles, though it's soft and not eager like my sister when she's vying for something of mine. "My dad took my sister and me to a convention in San Diego last year, and it was so much fun. I got to see the real Batmobile."

"You're lucky. I've always wanted to go. My dad would never take me to such a thing unless it was a bunch of doctors doing boring stuff."

Charlotte purses her lips. "Maybe, if my parents are both here for Christmas, I can ask them for a comic book just like this. Dad has been working a lot too, but he says it's because we need money. Maybe it's a bad idea to ask then."

My gaze is steady on the comic resting in my hands. Back at the store, the excitement of owning it and going against my dad was the reason for the impulse purchase.

But the longer I sit beside Charlotte, the more uncomfortable the tightness in my throat becomes. Then, I swallow the lump and know exactly what I need to do.

I extend my hand toward her. "Here, it's yours."

Charlotte's head flinches back slightly. "Mine?"

"Yeah, I've got plenty more comics in my future. You take it home."

Her small fingers reach out to take it from me, followed by eyes shining bright and her entire face lighting up with joy.

"Thank you, Alex," she whispers.

Standing up, I wipe the dirt off my sweats with a grin. I'm unable to hold back from doing something to make her happy. "Anytime, kid."

FIVE

The time when I moved back home

The sharp pain in my neck shoots up the back of my head when I move from the awkward position I find myself in.

Another day, another long night of studying.

The bad luck started when my alarm didn't go off at four this morning because of a blackout during the night. The early wake-up call was because we had to make the three-hour drive home with a U-Haul carrying most of our belongings from our one-bedroom apartment.

I'd finally convinced Sammy to move back to Carmel so I can work alongside my dad. She wasn't impressed when we weren't even an hour here, and Dad called me because the hospital was chaotic today.

It shouldn't have been a big deal until my body grew weary of the constant running around after idiotic patients who decided today was the day to take themselves to the ER. One woman stabbed herself with a sewing needle, which wasn't a big deal, but her fainting stressed out her husband who brought her in.

Then, there was the moron who decided to use his chainsaw while standing on a ladder. Lucky for him, the only thing he lost was his baby toe.

Dad sent me home when things quieted down, but it wasn't like I could rest. Sammy insisted I unpack, and my reluctance resulted in an argument before dinner.

The stress continues to mount, and so does the stupid pain inside my neck while I try to get some much-needed studying done.

Warm hands press against my shoulders as I close my eyes and welcome the relaxing massage.

"I'm sorry about before."

"It's been a long day for both of us," I tell her softly.

"You know, we haven't had a holiday in forever. Not since our honeymoon in Maui. Why don't we book something? We can use the break."

All my muscles tighten as I try to control my annoyance. Sammy is never happy unless we are living the life she *thinks* we can afford.

I move my shoulder to prompt her to stop touching me.

"We've gone over this."

"No, you said we had no money when I know we do," she argues back.

My body turns swiftly, so my eyes meet hers.

"The money we have is for a rainy day. You know, acting responsibly because we don't have a money tree growing in our backyard."

Sammy folds her arms in annoyance. "We're young... there's plenty of time to get more money."

"This is non-negotiable. End of story."

She shrugs with a bored expression. "Too late. I went

shopping today and bought a new bedroom suite since we're sleeping on the couch tonight."

My nostrils flare. "How much did you spend?"

"We'll make more money," she answers nonchalantly.

I grit my teeth while fixating on the screen to log into our bank account. The moment I set my eyes on the balance, my pulse speeds with heat flushing through my body.

"Are you fucking kidding me!"

"We have no bed nor suite to fill the large room. Beds are great for having sex. Remember how much sex we used to have?" she questions, then laughs.

"And you think an expensive bed will fix me getting you off?"

Sammy's smile disappears as her lips flatten with a flush of red spreading across her cheeks. Yeah, our sex life is redundant. She got me off when I needed it, and I got her off when she needed it. It wasn't often anymore, and to be honest, I'd rather jerk off to some video than deal with her anyway. Sex has become a chore. Couple it with a nagging wife, and I just can't be bothered.

I slam my book, looking at the time. "I've got an important assessment tomorrow and need to study. I'm going to my parents."

"Fine, whatever, Alex," she drags. Only now do I notice she's wearing the black dress I've told her is too short. "I'm going out anyway."

"Wearing that?" I question her.

"So now you care?"

"I've always cared about what my wife wears which is inappropriate. Put a jacket on."

I grab my books to shove into my bag. Without another word, I leave the house and jump into my car. The drive is short not giving me much time to dwell on tonight. I didn't even ask Sammy where she was going. I'm tired, defeated, and just need a moment away from her.

The lights are on inside my parents' house. Hopefully, I can avoid Adriana and not be distracted by her overbearing ways. As I exit the car with my bag over my shoulder, I fumble for my key and use it to open the back kitchen door.

My parents both lift their gaze to meet mine, surprised to see me.

"Alex," Mom calls softly. "Is everything okay? It's late."

"Yeah." I force a smile. "I just needed to concentrate and study, plus our sofa isn't big enough for me and Sammy to sleep on."

Dad purses his lips with his hands wrapped around his coffee mug.

"You need any help?"

"I think I got this, just need a different environment," I mumble. "I'm going to head to my room and stay over if that's okay."

"Alex, this will always be your home. You never have to ask."

"I know, Mom. Thanks."

I quickly run to my room, ignoring the music coming from Adriana's room. Fuck, she listens to crap.

As I turn on my light, I dump my bag and look around. Everything is just how I left it. Despite being away at college for many years, it's always good to be back home.

I don't waste any time turning my lamp on and getting my books out. With my headphones on, the music plays in my ears to drown out all the outside noise.

Hours pass, and I slowly grow weary. My eyes glance at the clock—

it's just past midnight. I lean back in my chair to stretch

my arms and crack my knuckles. I've hit my mental peak, knowing anything else I read from here on in will be pointless and not sink in.

The house is quiet with everyone asleep. I take a quick shower to warm my muscles, but a growl escapes my stomach making me hungry. Mom must have something in the refrigerator. This is the perks of living with a woman who knows how to cook.

Walking down the hallway, I make my way to the kitchen. Opening the refrigerator, Mom has some leftover casserole. I quickly heat it up, then eat out of the bowl.

I'm not feeling in the mood to sleep in my room, preferring the couch since it's softer, so I decide to head back to my room to grab my pillow and blanket first.

As I turn off the light, I hear a noise in front of me then crash into a female body.

The heated skin feels like nothing I've touched before, igniting some sort of reaction from me. It's not my sister or my mom, so my breathing stops with curiosity.

"Holy shit!" a girl's voice yells.

My body falls on top of hers, pinning her to the stairs. The unfamiliar scent is intoxicating, a perfume I've never smelled before. Beneath me, her body tenses up, and I can only assume it's a friend of Adriana's staying over.

A jolt of *something* shoots through me, causing a groan to escape my lips. I'm careful not to hurt her, pulling myself up to flick the light switch.

The familiar brown eyes blink at the sudden light, and it takes me a moment to realize it's Charlotte, all grown up.

"Charlotte?"

My eyes are drawn to how beautiful she has become. It's been years since I saw her last, so long I can't even recall.

"I'm so sorry, Alex," she answers in a squeaky voice, almost like she's affected by my presence.

Then, she reaches for the back of her head and winces. She must have hit it on the stairs. She rubs it gingerly, then lets out a small, "Ow."

"Are you okay? Come sit down."

I pull one of the stools out as she follows, then takes a seat. The lump needs to calm down, so I grab a bag of peas from the freezer and hold them against the lump. My height overpowers her, but then her warm breaths fall against my bare chest causing me to close my eyes at how good it feels. *Why the fuck am I feeling this, like butterflies or something?*

Then, I remember where I am and who I'm with.

"Better?" I ask, with a smile, as my eyes are drawn to her chest.

Fuck, she's not wearing a bra.

I do the math in my head. She's what ... eighteen?

Why are you even thinking about her age? Turn away now, stop staring at her perfectly shaped tits and hard nipples peeking through her tank.

Charlotte quickly folds her arms, noticing my perverted stare.

"Yes, thank you. I'm so sorry, I didn't realize you were here. Adriana didn't mention you had returned from college."

"I... um... came back this morning." I laugh, rubbing the back of my neck, unsure why since I'm the one caught staring at her tits. "She probably didn't tell you because she was too busy sucking face with that scrawny geek she's seeing. I didn't mean to startle you back there. I'm sleeping on the couch tonight because our bed hasn't arrived at our new place yet."

"Are you back here for good?" she asks with wide eyes.

"Not one-hundred percent sure, but in the meantime, I wanted to get some practical experience alongside my dad at the hospital. Plus, Samantha got a job at the gallery not too far from here, so yeah, I guess it keeps everyone happy," I explain, though not convincingly.

Charlotte nods, but then silence falls between us. Each time she avoids my stare, it allows me to examine her features more. Everything is so perfect—the warm color of her eyes, the shape of her nose, and the soft pink lips she doesn't realize she is biting.

"I better head back to bed." Charlotte hops off the stool, a little unsteady on her feet. "Adriana is making us go prom dress shopping tomorrow morning. What are the chances of her battery being tampered with, so the car won't start?"

"That's right, I forgot you aren't related to Donatella Versace like my sister claims she is." I grin.

My sister is a true pain in the ass, a diva as such. How she managed to convince my parents to convert a guest bedroom into a second wardrobe for her is beyond me. She doesn't even work, so I don't understand where she gets the money from because Dad can be tight. Clearly, Mom isn't.

Charlotte walks back to the stairs, but then she stops to turn around.

"It was nice seeing you again, Alex." She takes a few steps before stopping and turning around one more time. "And congratulations on your wedding. Adriana told me it was amazing."

And just like that, she disappears up the stairs leaving me alone with my thoughts.

I rub my face with my hands, trying to ignore whatever the fuck this weird sensation is spreading all over my body. So, she wasn't wearing a bra. All the women I watch in porn don't wear bras either—big fucking deal.

Then why can't you get her out of your head?

Suddenly, sleeping in the living room is less appealing. I need to be alone.

Back in my room, I choose to ignore the uncomfortable springs on my bed and turn off the light. The memory of Charlotte's innocent eyes and bare chest causes a stir inside my sweats. I toss and turn, trying to ignore the urge but it's begging me to pay attention.

No one has to know, just picture something else.

I wrap my hands around my cock, trying to picture Samantha down on her knees sucking my cock. The thought does nothing.

Then I see Charlotte's wide stare and the way she bites her lip. Each stroke sends a warm sensation across all of my body, and it takes me less than a minute to blow. My back arches into the mattress as my breathing is ragged.

Fuck, what have I done? Imagining another woman, an eighteen-year-old. Not just that, my sister's best friend.

Grabbing a tissue to wipe the cum off my stomach, I then dump the tissue into the trash can.

It's just a momentary lapse, that's it. I've done nothing wrong.

I eventually fall asleep but wake up at the crack of dawn. Charlotte's the first thing that comes to my mind. I can't see her again, not until I control whatever the fuck my dick was doing last night. It doesn't mean though, I can't help her with the problem of my psychotic sister.

Quickly, I get changed, brush my teeth, and then run downstairs to see Mom already in the kitchen.

"Good morning, Alex," she greets, prompting me to sit down and eat. I glance at the time knowing my sister will be asleep for at least another two hours. "Sleep well?"

"Sort of," I mumble.

Mom's gaze focuses on me with a worried expression. "Is everything okay?"

"Just a lot on, you know. Samantha is just too much to handle right now."

"Marriage is hard, Alex. It's not always perfect. She moved here per your wishes so maybe you need to be patient with her."

My head tilts with annoyance. "Did she tell you to say that?"

"No, Alex. Just a mother's observations."

I bite into a piece of toast, then drink the coffee Mom poured. My eyes keep glancing toward the stairs, reliving last night.

"So, what's the deal with Charlotte? Does she stay here a lot?"

Mom sits across from me, drinking her coffee.

"You could say that. She's had a tough time with her mother in and out."

The memory of the comic book incident comes to mind. It was such a long time ago, so long I'd forgotten about it.

"That's still going on?" I question, surprised.

Mom nods. "Like I said earlier, marriage is hard, Alex. I don't ask questions, but I know Charlotte is strong. She doesn't deserve to be going through her parents' battles, so the best thing we can do is offer her a place when she needs it."

Glancing at the time on my watch, I remember my plan. Inside the drawer under the counter is some stationery Mom keeps in case we need it. Sliding my chair out, I open the drawer and grab the Post-it note and pen to write a message.

"By the way, Dad mentioned something about Adriana's car playing up," I lie, though with good intentions behind it. "I'm going to get it checked out because I know Dad is busy."

Mom smiles. "Thank you, Alex. Your father's already left for surgery. I'm glad you're finally thinking about your sister."

I lean in, kissing Mom on the cheek, then grab Adriana's keys.

"Anything for my sister," I answer, closing the door behind me with a smirk on my face.

SIX

The time when Charlotte went on birth control

The moment I ran into Charlotte inside my parents' kitchen, my life changed.

My heart started beating differently.

My mind became consumed with only the thought of Charlotte.

I tried to fight the feelings, desperately reminding myself every moment I took a breath of my vows needing to remain intact. In front of my family, friends, and God's presence, I made Samantha my wife.

But I could no longer fight.

Every moment with Charlotte only made me desire her more. The force it's unexplainable. Its power is nothing like I've experienced before. Love, lust, and everything two souls find when the connection is so strong, you know it was always meant to be.

Our first kiss—broke me.

In a good way.

And now, I'm living a double life.

The throbbing inside my head refuses to pass despite my earlier effort to consume two Advil. I'd followed with a strong coffee to keep me going for the remainder of the day.

It had been another one of those nights.

Sammy came home in a mood, but I argued back instead of ignoring her like usual until she demanded I stay away from her. It didn't last long for her to beg me to sleep in our bed, to which I refused. The couch has been my choice of late, another reason she felt compelled to argue our marriage is nothing but a sham.

How could I argue? My thoughts were consumed by Charlotte. The mere idea of my wife touching me felt wrong. There is only one person I can't stop thinking about, but of course, the guilt eats away at me every single fucking moment I'm awake.

It's a deadly companion built on shame and selfish principles.

The phone rings inside the small office. My head is buried in paperwork, my least favorite thing about studying medicine. I ignore the noise with the need to focus until Dr. Hanson announces he must attend to a patient. The clinic hasn't stopped all day, and even he looks worn out after the multiple coffees he has drunk since I clocked on for my shift.

The silence from his departure is welcoming, allowing me to focus on a patient's file, but it's short-lived as he re-enters.

"Alex, would you mind sitting in on this consult. It's pretty straightforward, and frankly, we can make it quick as I can use the break."

"Of course, Dr. Hanson. What's the visit for?"

Dr. Hanson adjusts his glasses, reading the file in front of him. "A young girl is looking to go on birth control."

"Smart move," I say, closing the file I'd been reading. "And the patient's name?"

"Charlotte..." he begins at the same time my eyes flick toward him, "... Mason."

The corners of my mouth slowly quirk up, but then I force myself to remain professional, reverting to a blank expression.

Things between us changed the night after Adriana's birthday. A simple kiss became so much more. I'd only wish Charlotte didn't overhear the argument between Samantha and me the morning after. It wasn't my finest moment, but perhaps the truth unveiling itself forced our feelings to the surface. Denial can only go so far, and frankly—I am tired of fighting the truth.

And from our admission inside the pool house, things got heated quickly. I still remember yesterday when she was supposed to be studying with Adriana at my parents' house, but Adriana bailed to go see Elijah ...

Adriana slams the door, telling us she'll be back in an hour. I had no idea Charlotte would be here as I only planned to stop by to pick up a book from Dad's office.

The big brown eyes stare at me inside the kitchen, but then they fall to the countertop in a sudden move. Charlotte's cheeks turn a perfect shade of crimson, and if possible, making her all the more beautiful even though she's still in her school uniform.

"Alex?" she barely manages, clearing her throat to control her shaky voice. "I didn't know you'd be here."

I do my best to hide my smirk, crossing my arms with a persistent stare instead.

"I had to pick something up. You know, since it's my parents' house."

"Uh, yeah, of course."

The bottom of my lip angles while biting the side, trying to hold back the urge to touch her. Yet the forbidden fruit is dangled in front of me, demanding I have just one taste.

I run my hands through my hair, then take steps toward Charlotte to grab her hand. The moment our fingers touch, the adrenaline runs inside my veins, causing my heart to pump hard beneath my shirt.

Charlotte's eyes meet mine, the innocence behind the brown orbs begging me to take the lead. I pull on her hand, tilting my head to motion for her to follow me.

We walk toward my bedroom on the second floor, a few doors down from my sister's room. I place my hand on the knob, turning it to smell the familiar scent of cologne my mother gifts me every Christmas.

"So, umm, this is your room?" Charlotte asks while taking it all in.

"You've never seen my room?"

"Not technically, I mean, a few times Adria—" She stops speaking while her eyes widen.

"Adriana, what?"

"Uh, never mind."

"You can't say never mind," I chastise, letting go of her hand and folding my arms. "Why does my sister snoop in my room?"

"Look, I don't want to get involved in sibling drama," she declares while staring at the pinboard hanging above my desk. "Let's just say she was short of funds and thought she could find some lying here."

"As usual," I grunt, annoyed at my sister.

Charlotte raises her hand to touch a photo pinned to the corkboard. I move in closer to see it's my high school graduation.

"It feels like a lifetime ago," I mumble, glancing at the

cap and gown I'm wearing. "My dad gave me this stern lecture of all his high hopes and how I better not screw it up."

"You didn't," Charlotte whispers. "You won't."

I place my arms around her waist, bringing her close to me. The smell of her hair is sweet, like strawberries mixed with vanilla, but a scent so pure it only reminds me of her.

My lips find their way to her neck, kissing her skin gently as her breathing becomes louder.

"We shouldn't be in here," Charlotte warns.

"Adriana won't be back for a while."

"If we get caught ...."

I pull back slightly, enough to turn her around, so her face is only a breath away from mine.

"Are you scared?" I ask while glancing at her lips, desperate to kiss her, wanting to lay her on my bed.

Charlotte places her hands flat on my chest. "I'm scared of a lot of things. Your sister finding out, my dad finding out, and of course, your wife finding out."

Slowly, I tilt my head so our lips are only inches apart.

"They won't."

"How do you know, Alex?"

The truth is, I don't know anything. But the last thing I want is for Charlotte to walk away and tell me she can't do this. The thought alone brings a wave of nausea like the air has been sucked from my lungs, and I can't breathe without her.

And right now, I need to ease her worry.

I cup her face with my hands, guiding her mouth onto mine. Her warm lips part, allowing me to taste her without any resistance. A soft moan escapes her, causing my dick to stir beneath my jeans. Fuck, control yourself.

My hands fall from her face, sliding down to her waist,

where I drag her to my bed and pull her down. I watch her chest rise and fall as I lay on top of her.

"I'm not a virgin," she reminds me.

"I know," I answer with a forced smile. "I was there when my sister blurted it out."

"Oh, I forgot."

My body presses against her, forcing her legs apart. Then, my hands wander to the hem of her navy skirt, toying with the edge of the fabric as she waits in anticipation. Just as I'm about to slide my hand between her legs, the sound of a car catches my attention.

I jump off Charlotte, racing to the window to see my mom's car.

"Shit, it's my mom," I tell Charlotte. "Go to Adriana's room, and I'll say you fell asleep since Adriana had to step out."

Charlotte's eyes widen as she nods in silence. She quickly stands up, adjusts her skirt, then takes a deep breath. She reaches for the door, but I pull her back toward me, leaning in for one more kiss.

"Just so you know, I wouldn't have fucked you here."

The corners of her lips curve upward. "And just so you know, Alex. I'm not the type of girl to give in so easily."

Dr. Hanson places his hand on the doorknob, twisting it without much effort as I follow behind him. The door opening catches Charlotte off guard, causing the plastic heart she's obviously touched to fall out of her hands and onto the floor.

Her long brown hair falls past her shoulders as she leans forward to retrieve it at the same time I do. Then, I watch her body tense—the stiffening of her shoulders to the way her entire body freezes on the spot.

Swiftly, her eyes are drawn to mine, riddled with panic as they widen in my presence.

Dr. Hanson takes a seat, quick to bring out his notes. "Charlotte, this is my intern, Dr. Alex Edwards. Now, let's continue our discussion. Are you sexually active?"

Charlotte barely manages to make it to the plastic chair across from us. Unable to look at me, she plays with the loose frays from the rip in her jeans. Her simple white tank and jeans only make her look more beautiful—perfect and simple, enhancing her natural features.

The color of her cheeks quickly changes to crimson, the same color as yesterday when I found her inside my parents' kitchen.

"Umm, yes ... I mean, no ... maybe," she barely manages to answer.

"Perhaps I need to rephrase my question," Dr. Hanson continues softly. "Have you had sexual intercourse?"

"Yes."

"More than once?"

"Yes," she replies faintly.

"How many sexual partners have you had?"

Her posture falls, almost as if she's trying to retreat into a dark hole where I'm not

watching her with a smirk on my face.

"Only one."

"Will you be continuing to have sexual intercourse with this person?"

"Definitely not," she blurts out.

Dr. Hanson writes notes on his notepad. "Did you use protection such as condoms?"

Her eyes momentarily meet mine, but she's quick to turn away from embarrassment.

"Yes, Dr. Hanson."

"That's a very responsible attitude, Charlotte. I understand these questions seem personal. However, it's my responsibility to ensure you're educated on everything associated with being sexually active," Dr. Hanson informs her, then continues while she shuffles her feet nervously. "I'm guessing your intention is to be intimate with a specific person at this stage. Charlotte, how much do you know of their sexual history?"

Suddenly, her posture straightens, and the shy girl sitting inside this room glances at me with new confidence.

"To be honest, I think he's slept around ... a lot," she answers with raised brows.

The smirk on my face dwindles. Sure, back in my early years, I slept around because I had the freedom to do so. But then, I started dating Sammy. She was wild in the bedroom, which I somehow misinterpreted as marriage material.

My family warned me of being too young to commit. But of course, I didn't fucking listen. Marriage seemed like the easy way out. How very wrong of me to come to that conclusion.

The truth is, I've barely touched my wife in the last few months. The more she nags about babies and wanting more money, the less attracted to her I have become.

And since the moment I crashed into Charlotte inside my parents' hallway, I've made excuses as to why we haven't fucked like an ordinary husband and wife.

"Is he still behaving this way?" Dr. Hanson asks with concern in his eyes.

"No, he's with someone long-term."

"Is he still sexually active with her?"

"I'm not sure, Dr. Hanson. He is a man, after all," Charlotte responds with coldness in her tone.

I beg her with my eyes to trust me. If only I could reassure her the only person I want naked in my bed is the person sitting in front of me.

"I strongly suggest you use both condoms and the pill. Sexually transmitted diseases are easier to catch than you may think." He scribbles some notes and hands the chart to me. "Everything looks good to me. I'll leave you with Dr. Edwards to check your blood pressure and write up your prescription. It was nice to meet you, Charlotte."

Dr. Hanson quickly exits the room leaving the two of us. I retrieve the blood pressure cuff from the table and wrap it around her arm, strapping it on while grinning.

"So, I'm a player, am I?"

"More like a manwhore," she drags, then sighs heavily. "I hate you right now ... you know that, right?"

"Aww, no, you don't. You love me right now. Otherwise, why would you be here getting a prescription for the pill in case your sexual activity picks up?"

She shakes her head, covering her face in embarrassment. "You're a jerk."

I remove the blood pressure cuff, then write her result on the chart in front of me. Placing it down on the table, I wheel my chair closer, so I can reach out and touch her.

"Since when do you work here?" she questions while relaxing her shoulders. "I thought you just interned at the hospital?"

"They were short-staffed..." I pause before grabbing a lock of her hair and pushing it behind her ear. I'll find any excuse to touch her, feeding my obsession at any cost.

"So, tell me, Charlotte, are we doing this?"

"This?"

I choose my words carefully, needing her to know this is more than two young people jumping into bed for fun. The moment I'm inside her, no one else will ever compare. The thought alone terrifies me, yet it's everything I want.

"You came here today to make sure you were protected. That we are protected."

"I just wanted to make sure, you know ... just in case."

I'm breaking all the rules now, playing with fire and compromising a patient for my own selfish needs. I lean over, locking the door behind Charlotte. Then, without a second thought, my lips find their way onto hers.

Her soft moan inside our heated kiss only confirms exactly how I feel. There is no turning back on this path we've found ourselves on. I want her, and nothing will stop me.

Not even the wife I chose for better or for worse.

In sickness and in health.

Til' death us do part.

"I've never wanted anything more, Charlotte. You have to believe me."

She places her arms around my neck, reassuring me she feels the same way. Inside her touch, everything feels right despite all the odds facing us.

"I believe you. And anyway, if it wasn't your words that told me, it's the general saluting me right now."

I place my forehead against hers. "You're crazy."

"Insane is the word you are looking for," she corrects.

A small laugh escapes me. Then, I unlock the door, careful we aren't caught by anyone. I grab the notepad and rip the paper off to hand to her.

"Here you go, Miss Mason. The reason you came. Hope you have fun," I tease playfully.

Charlotte winks. "Thank you, Dr. Edwards. I'm sure the pleasure won't be all mine."

And just like that, we sealed our fate.

It's only a matter of time before I'm inside Charlotte and claiming her as mine.

SEVEN

The time we got drunk under the bleachers

I'd lost my virginity in high school at the age of sixteen to a cheerleader. I was a junior, not genuinely understanding sex nor what it entailed besides blowing at the end. Sex was so casually thrown around that it wasn't a big deal. Of course, it didn't help that most girls in school were loose and willing to spread their legs for any jock.

In college, it was the same. The only difference was the freedom to have sex because of dorm rooms and the lack of supervision. At the time, I wasn't complaining. I slept around, almost jeopardizing my grades because pussy was more important.

It made me feel like a man.

From a young age, it'd been ingrained into us that college was a sexual awakening. Movies, television shows, and books—all of which painted this lifestyle of freedom and exploration into adulthood. Then, I met Samantha, and my views changed. Yes, she was wild, but being in a relationship gave me a sort of comfort I'd never experienced.

When you're comfortable with someone, you allow yourself to explore, which is another experience altogether.

With Charlotte—everything feels entirely new. Like a fire inside me has ignited, and I'm unable to control the roaring flames from spreading into a catastrophic wildfire.

There were too many close calls.

Too many near instances because I was greedy and wanted Charlotte every waking moment.

After the night at the hotel when we first had sex, I needed her every single fucking day. She has become my addiction like a drug I can't get out of my system but need to survive.

Today is no different.

Samantha gave me this long spiel on how our dining room looked so drab, and shopping for new furniture plus accessories would make her happy. I argued for a hot minute to continue the charade and then gave in. It was difficult, given she's been draining our bank account. Yet, the guilt ate away at me, so I said nothing. Finally, she mentioned driving to San Jose and making a strong point about her absence until late tonight. So, I knew we had time.

Charlotte is standing beside me in the small foyer inside my house. Still wearing her school uniform, she stops in her tracks until I grab her hand and lead her into the living room.

"Do you think anyone saw us?" she asks, worried as usual.

"No," I mumble while kissing her neck. Her back is pressed against my chest, so I slide my hand beneath her school shirt, desperate to touch her.

She doesn't say another word, allowing me to squeeze her perky tits while I harden against her. Charlotte arches her head back, but then her muscles stiffen just as I'm about to lift her skirt and fuck her bent over on the couch.

Her hands clutch mine, moving them away so she can distance herself.

"We can't here."

"Okay," I answer calmly. "Then come to the bedroom."

Charlotte turns to face me, raising her arms to fold them beneath her chest. She bares her teeth with bulging eyes to warn me she's angry with my suggestion.

"In your bed?" she questions with grit. "The same bed you sleep in with your wife?"

With a small sigh escaping me, I try not to anger her further despite my annoyance over the same argument. No matter how many times I reassure her nothing is going on, she circles back to the same thing.

"C'mon, you know I don't fuck her. I've told you that repeatedly."

"Why should I believe you?" Charlotte draws her brows with a resenting stare. "You do sleep in the same bed with her? She does try to lean over and touch you. I'm sure she's tried multiple times to get you to fuck her, and of course, you just want to shut her up."

I run my hands through my hair, pinching my lips together with a clenched jaw.

"What the fuck, Charlotte? I'm sick of having this same argument. I promise you I don't fuck her, end of the story."

"Yeah, well, I'm sick of sneaking around and being the sidepiece," she mutters.

It's clear her being here has only soured her mood. It's not the first time she's visited my house, but the last time, it was under different circumstances.

It's a Friday afternoon, and from what she said earlier, her dad won't be home until late. I don't want to risk being caught by her dad. Mark Mason would *kill* me on the spot. So, I do the next best thing.

"Let's get out of here," I tell her, grabbing my keys.

"Where are we going?"

"Will you stop asking questions and just trust me for once?"

Charlotte remains quiet, then follows me but stops shy of the liquor cabinet. She opens the glass door, removing a bottle of Patrón.

"Okay, let's go," she says with a grin.

A deep sigh escapes me, knowing we can get into big trouble if we're caught and Charlotte has been drinking.

"Look, you're underage and shouldn't be drinking."

She cocks her head with a stubborn gaze. "Yeah, and I shouldn't be fucking my best friend's older brother either."

There is no point arguing with her, so I don't. As I open the front door, my eyes quickly scan outside to make sure no one sees us. We get into my car, but then I remember the tequila. If we drink, I can't drive. The last thing I need is a DUI and losing my medical license. Abruptly, I turn off the engine.

"We're walking," I inform her.

Charlotte rolls her eyes and then lets out an annoyed huff. "Great."

About three blocks from my house is a soccer field. It's only used on weekends, so given it's a late Friday afternoon, it should be empty. The walk to the field is through the bush, which is convenient so no one can see us.

When the field is in sight, it's empty with not a single person around. I grab her hand to lead and take her under the bleachers. It's a bit of an effort to get under, given my height.

"Okay, sit," I command.

Charlotte sits on the grassy patch as I yank the bottle from her. Twisting the lid open, I pour a shot for myself, downing it in one go. It burns, having been a while since I've drunk this stuff straight. Then, giving myself a moment to let it settle, I pour half the amount and hand it to Charlotte.

"Really? I'm not a kid."

"Fine." I pour more to her satisfaction.

She quickly takes it from me, tossing it back without hesitation. Her face reacts instantly, scowling followed by a rasp from the aftertaste.

"That hurt. We should have brought lemons and salt."

"Tequila is supposed to hurt," I tease, running my thumb against her bottom lip. "Until you're numb, then the life of the party. Next, you'll forget everything until tomorrow when everything hurts, and you question your will to live."

Without giving her a chance to respond, I move in closer, demanding she sit on top of me. Charlotte's legs wrap around my waist at the same time, and her arms lace the back of my neck. Her warm breath spreads across my skin as her lips inch close before she kisses me deeply.

Our tongues battle in a frenzy while soft moans escape her. My hands move beneath Charlotte's skirt to cup her ass inside her panties. A groan rumbles inside me, desperate to fuck her right here and now.

"Here?" She pants.

"Why not?"

She pulls away, trying to catch her breath. "What if someone sees us?"

I move my fingers deeper into her panties, brushing against her clit. "Okay, I'll wait for you to beg me to fuck you then."

She's drenched, and I know her body so well—every curve, every inch of her heated pussy. At a slow and agonizing pace, my fingers glide in and out, drowning in the warmth of her arousal. Then, I remove them to place them in my mouth, tasting her like it's my last meal on Earth.

"You taste sweet," I tease with a smirk playing on my lips.

"Fuck me now, please," she begs, desperately smashing her lips onto mine, just like I knew she would.

I yank her panties aside, trying to unbuckle my jeans at the same time. When my cock springs free, it doesn't take her long to slide herself on.

And every single time she does, it feels like fucking *heaven*.

Charlotte pushes her hips down, taking me all in. Her face is expressive as every inch enters her, a beautiful sight to watch because I'm large, and it reaches to parts she's never imagined possible.

I watch her with a delicious stare, riding me slowly at a pace that drives me insane. Her long brown hair flows down her back as she throws her head backward. I'm fixated on every move and expression, trying my best not to blow right now. *It's too soon. Control yourself.* I'm forced to clench my jaw and close my eyes for a moment, enough to slow down my body to last a few more minutes, at best.

Charlotte is fucking perfect.

The way her body moves, how our bodies move together in sync. The sound of her soaking wet pussy as she braces herself to come any moment now.

My lips find hers in desperation. Then, she pulls back with a smile on her face, slowing down. She grabs the tequila bottle beside us but doesn't use the cap this time.

With her hands, she moves my jaw to open my mouth.

Then free pours into my mouth. Before I swallow, she moves her tongue inside, tasting the burning liquor with me but continues to ride me slowly.

Fuck. Me.

My hands fumble with her shirt in a frenzy, unbuttoning it quickly because I need to suck on her tits right now. With her chest exposed, I unclasp her bra, then yank it down brutally.

I fucking love her tits. The perfect shape and size, perky and young. Her nipples stand hard, teasing me so effortlessly. I move my mouth in, grazing my teeth against her nipples which causes her to ache in delight.

Charlotte deserves to be worshiped, so I take turns sucking on one side while fondling the other. Her hands run through my hair as she arches back and warns me she's about to come.

My mouth pulls away so I can watch her. The veins on her neck are prominent against her delicate skin. Every muscle tightens as goosebumps form all over her body. Charlotte begs me not to stop while her moaning becomes a low-rumbling hum as she still rides me.

I grip her ass to help her grind against me as she weakens from the rush she's just experienced. It's enough for me to finish, my hands gripping her neck as I allow the sensation to wash over me.

Bursts of light blind me, the sensation ripping across my entire body, making it difficult to breathe. It's always like this between us, a euphoric ending to our maddening affair. The forbidden tryst we've found ourselves in has turned into this unexplainable force that intensifies each time we sneak around to feed our desires.

"Oh, God," Charlotte expels with a ragged breath. "That was..."

"Satisfying?" I smirk, also trying to catch my breath.

A grin widens across her flushed face. "Amazing."

I remain inside her, wanting to stay like this even if my dick tells me it's over. So far, he's obeying and staying hard. *Greedy mother fucker.*

As I take a swig from the bottle, Charlotte throws her head back again. Finally, she opens her eyes, taking the bottle from me, but this time drinking it with much more ease.

"Don't stop," she begs.

My hands run down her back, memorizing every groove like keys on a piano. How can she be so fucking beautiful? If only we had met at a different time before I married Samantha. Then, the guilt crashes over me like a tidal wave. I reach for the bottle, almost emptying the contents to numb the lingering thoughts.

"You know what I've fantasized about..." Charlotte trails off mid-moan.

"Me fucking this sweet ass of yours?"

She quickly shifts her gaze onto me with a teasing smile. "Fucking you in an elevator."

"Hmmm... I know the maintenance guy, Joe, who works in the hospital. I'm sure I can arrange there to be some sort of technical difficulty resulting in the elevator stopping for like ten minutes."

"Ten minutes? You wouldn't last that long," she muses.

I grab the back of Charlotte's head to draw her mouth to mine. With a deep kiss, I thrust my cock inside her at the same time, desperate to taste her delicious groan.

"Such a smart mouth on you," I warn with a sneer. "And you think you could?"

"I never said I would," she corrects me. "I just said I want to fuck you in an elevator."

"And what about me?"

Charlotte tilts her head, trying to suppress her smile. "Let me guess. You want to circle back the convo about you fucking me in the ass?"

My hands move down her waist to cup her perfectly rounded ass cheeks. With a tight grip, I spread them apart, which causes her to gasp.

"Don't be scared," I say softly. "I'll be gentle."

I drown myself in Charlotte's longing stare before she nods in silence. *Fuck, okay, I need to calm down and be gentle.*

My lips find their way to her neck as I spread soft kisses while pulling out at the same time. Each kiss trails her skin until I lower my head and take her nipples back in my mouth. This time, I'm not so rough and tease gently to relax her body.

When satisfied she's relaxed enough, I lean into her ear and whisper, "Turn around."

Without a word, she shuffles so her ass is facing me. Unable to control my urges, I bite down on my lip with sheer force, almost tasting blood, before resting my palms on her cheeks.

Charlotte begins to tense again, so I move my left hand between her legs and teasingly start rubbing her clit.

"Oh, God," she gasps, pushing her ass into me. "I'm ready."

My heart suddenly begins to race from the nerves. It's not because I haven't fucked a woman in the ass. In fact, I've done it several times. The difference is those women, including Samantha, were used to it and didn't mind it rough. Therefore, I wasn't gentle in the act.

This is different. I'm scared to hurt her, worried I'll inflict pain because of my selfish fantasies. She's never had a man in her ass, and the pressure makes me question whether I should go ahead.

Before I can get in a word, she reaches behind her, begins to stroke my cock, and then brings it to her entrance.

Okay, stop overthinking this.

Just take it slow.

I purposely spit on my shaft to create a lubricant, spreading it on the tip of my cock before I enter. To ease the pain for her, I rub the small of her back as I focus and begin entering. My senses are hyperaware, listening out for her sounds as well as focusing on her body's reactions.

Only the tip is in, and I feel her body tense while she takes deep breaths. My hand reaches for her clit again, rubbing it in a circular motion until she sinks into me. Charlotte's moans heighten, prompting me to push deeper while making sure she is okay.

As soon as I'm completely in, I stop to give her a moment to breathe. When I think she can't handle it, Charlotte slowly rocks back and forth at her own pace. Fuck, she's tight, and I'm barely holding on.

"*Deeper,*" she begs.

I obey her commands, though I continue at a slow pace not to hurt her. We find ourselves moving so effortlessly, and she warns me again she's about to come, but then a brutal ring interrupts us. I slow down, glancing over at her phone.

"Cockblocker," I mumble when I see it's my sister.

"I'll call her back later."

I glance over again for some sick and twisted reason as a smirk plays on my lips.

"No, answer it."

Charlotte snorts. "You're inside my ass, and you want me to answer it?"

"I dare you."

I'm expecting Charlotte to ignore me, so when she reaches over for the phone and answers hello, I know the tequila has loosened her inhibitions.

"I'm kinda busy, Adriana. Whatever your emergency is, it can wait."

My hands grip her waist as I continue to slide in and out of her, enjoying the choke in her voice when she speaks.

"Whatever car for prom is fine. If it fits everyone, just book it," she continues with a clenched jaw.

This time, I spread her cheeks to get a good look at my cock entering her. Fuck, I'm ready to blow. So, what if I go first? I'll make sure she comes right after me. My movements pick up, as does my tight grip on her waist. I have this desperate need to slap her ass, and just because I want to, I pull my hand back and then slap my palm against her cheek for it to make a loud sound.

"Adriana, I have to go, bye," Charlotte rushes, then hits end call and throws the phone away from us. "I'm going to come now!"

Her blissful finish tightens around my cock, causing me to blow inside her ass while I shut my eyes and try to catch my breath. The sensation reaches every part of me until my limbs feel like jelly, and I'm unable to move a single muscle.

Our ragged breathing echoes under the bleachers, and slowly, I pull myself out as she whimpers.

"You beat me to it," I tease.

"Yeah, well, you're the jerk who tried to come while his sister was rambling about cars for prom."

Charlotte turns around, then collapses to the ground on her back. Her chest rises and falls, still unable to stabilize her breathing.

"A jerk you still love, right?"

Her hand caresses my cheek as the corners of her eyes crinkle with a smile accompanying it. A silent moment passes between us, but I've learned during our time together that being silent isn't bad. Silence gives us the opportunity to speak the words our heart is sometimes afraid to say out loud.

"Always and forever," she finally whispers.

EIGHT

The time I became a billionaire

The empty glass of scotch sits on the table beside me.

It's an expensive bottle, aged to perfection and gifted from a client as a thank you. Receiving gifts isn't out of the ordinary, but at least this gift is useful, unlike the other worthless crap people think I'll enjoy.

The bottle is half empty, sitting on the glass table of this drab hotel room. I've always despised airport hotels' bland interiors and ridiculously small square footage. Sure, it's supposed to be a place just to crash, but why not sleep in style.

You're almost a billionaire. Make it happen.

Billionaire—the word has a delicious ring to it. The power and control lure me in with promises of a better life.

My eyes glance toward my watch to note the time. I need to leave soon to board my flight to London. I'd done this route many times, but this time it's for good.

The last three years have been under my grandfather's watch. Everything I've learned is because of him.

Alfred Edwards is a mogul, yet to me, he was just the grandfather who would shower me with presents on my birthday and Christmas. Occasionally, he would visit, much to my father's annoyance.

I barely knew the man, though he always made an effort to be friendly and ask me questions about my interests, such as sports.

Then, it all changed.

He paid me a visit one night after I'd left Samantha. It wasn't a great night. I was alone and miserable with a job at the hospital I started to lose interest in. I'm not sure who informed him of my miseries, or maybe his timing was just right.

It was an offer I couldn't refuse to step into his position of Chairman. At first, I declined the offer, not knowing much about business since I'd studied medicine. Yet, he offered to shadow his steps and to give as much time as needed to learn the role.

At this time, I had no idea he had been diagnosed with colorectal cancer. He hadn't appeared sick or showed any signs of the illness.

But he knew his mortality, and he refused to give away all his hard work to money-grabbing leeches who weren't family.

Alfred Edwards wanted his legacy to live on.

My life, from that moment, changed forever.

With this newfound power came a new existence. I thrived on money and everything it represented. I wasn't afraid to own the boardroom nor let anyone control my actions. I'm no longer indebted to any woman. At least, none who will destroy me.

My thoughts run rampant, so I decide to get out of this hell hole and straight to the airport. It's better to be surrounded by strangers and noise than to wallow in self-pity like I'm a fool trapped in mistakes.

JFK is busy as usual, with people running around in chaos, trying to rush to the gates to make their flight. I'm glad to have time on my hands, leisurely taking each step without the stress of the announcements blaring over the PA system.

My stay in Manhattan had been short, just a few days to tie up some loose ends before London. There was an opportunity to stay long-term in Manhattan, but I wasn't in the mood to live on the East Coast. A part of me just wanted to be anywhere but here.

It takes a good thirty minutes to clear security, even with my business class ticket. With my passport and ticket in hand, I make my way to the gate and straight to the priority passengers' line.

"Flight 789 to London to now boarding priority passengers. Please come forward to board the flight," the hostess announces over the speaker.

I grab the handle of the small black carry-on suitcase beside me and form part of the short line.

London. A faraway place, but a chance to forget about my past and the nightmares which plague me. Of late, the nightmares have reoccurred almost every night. Coincidently, this only happens in Manhattan, which is odd since I'd never been here with her to be able to create any memories.

Her... I can't even say her fucking name anymore.

The line moves quickly from checking our boarding passes to walking down the ramp to the front of the plane. I stop as some passengers make small talk with the captain and hostess.

When I'm finally at the front, I give a simply nod as the hostess eyes me like a piece of candy. She's not bad, but I'm not in the mood. Something about this trip is bothering me, and the last thing I need is pussy.

Maybe that's exactly what you need.

The seating area has pod-style cubicles, which is great for ignoring everyone else. Reaching down, I lift my suitcase and slide it into the overhead compartment above me. Then, I take a seat and get myself settled.

My eyes shift toward the tarmac outside the window, gazing with a heaviness inside my chest.

It's been four years.

A long time, or maybe too little time to move on from the past.

I wonder where she is, what she's doing. She isn't back home, nor has she been for the last four years. My parents still owned their home, and I'm certain my mother would have told my sister, who then would have mentioned something to me.

After Adriana and I visited her mother, it was clear I was to stay away. She had moved on.

My Charlotte had found happiness elsewhere.

On occasion, I toyed with the idea of hiring a private investigator, but what would I say even if I found her? The damage is done. If I saw her with another man, I wouldn't be able to control my jealousy. All it'd do is make her resent me even more. No matter what I do, I'm the loser in all of this.

The phone rings inside my pocket, forcing me to retrieve it to answer. My gaze falls upon the caller ID as I expel a small grunt before answering.

"Yes," is all I say.

"I didn't get a chance to say goodbye to you," Adriana whines.

"I was busy."

"C'mon, Alex."

"Don't call me that."

"Sorry, Lex." I almost hear her roll her eyes. "I wish you would have stopped by to see our place. You were only a cab ride away."

Adriana had recently graduated with Elijah, and they moved in together. For every milestone she's reached, I thought about Charlotte. Somewhere out there, she would have graduated.

I choose not to acknowledge Adriana's comment. The last four years have been strained between us. I'm not innocent. It's because every time I'm with Adriana, I half-expect to see Charlotte by her side. I knew I had to distance myself when it all became too much.

"Listen, I need to go."

"Lex?" Adriana calls.

My hand moves toward my face as I pinch the bridge of my nose in frustration. "Yes."

"Good luck in London. I hope you find what you're looking for."

The call ends, leaving me to ponder on her last comment.

What I'm looking for are peace and quiet. A break from the guilt which eats away at me every day I wake up. I'm done fighting these demons, ready for change and a life of solitude that will suit me just fine.

And just as quickly as the call ended, the plane took off into the sky for my next journey.

My assistant, Kate, holds the large boardroom doors open as I walk in, dressed in a new Armani suit.

Kate started only yesterday, and so far, no complaints on my end. She's young but obeys my commands and doesn't appear threatened like the other pathetic employees who run and hide the moment I step into the office.

Inside the boardroom, everyone stands at my arrival. Most of them I know from my previous visits. All but one man who stands on my right.

"Bentley James Woods," he introduces while extending his hand.

I shake his hand politely. "Lex Edwards."

Everyone takes a seat as I promptly start the meeting. The time goes fast as meetings do when there's a lot to cover. Before I know it, it's after five, and everyone is ready to call it a day. Not me since my working days usually end close to midnight. It's not like I have a family or partner to go home to, so why not work hard and make more money.

"So, you up for a pint tonight?" Bentley asks, catching me by surprise.

"A pint," I repeat, rubbing my chin. "I guess I better get used to this English slang."

Bentley pats my shoulder with a chuckle. "Bloody yanks, it's like nothing exists outside of America. What ya need is a pub and a good pint to call it a day."

I welcome Bentley's humor. It beats all the boring chit-chat from the other executives sitting in the room.

"A pub and pint sound good, Bentley," I tell him.

He nods with a smile. "By the way, call me BJ. It's less

formal, and Bentley is also my father's name. I'd rather no association with him."

The corners of my lips curve upward into a slight smirk. It appears I'm not the only person who doesn't have a nurturing relationship with their father.

"BJ, interesting choice of initials," I muse.

BJ leans over, quickly checking to make sure Kate has left the room. "Don't be fooled, mate. It's a conversation starter with women and equates to exactly that, a blow job."

A small chuckle escapes me. "Maybe London isn't so bad."

With a knowing grin, BJ closes his laptop. "You're in good hands. Trust me, you're going to see another side to this town you never knew existed."

NINE

The time I finally held her in my arms

The moment my eyes set on Charlotte inside the busy Manhattan restaurant, I knew why I'd fought for so long to stay alive.

My reason for breathing was sitting at the table beside me. She was no longer the young girl I'd left behind all those years ago. Charlotte had grown into a very beautiful woman.

A beautiful woman who committed herself to another man with the plan to marry him and create a life together.

A life that was always meant to be with *me*.

Many things in my life made sense, and a lot defied the odds.

London was my home, and these trips to Manhattan had become a regular occurrence, much to my annoyance. This trip, in particular, was close to being canceled. BJ pushed me to meet with stakeholders, suspecting foul play and insisted my presence was needed.

I sometimes wonder what would have happened if I

didn't go on the trip. Would I have ever run into her in this lifetime? Would she have gone ahead and married him, given him children? And what would have been left of me?

The universe tested me. Our past affair saw Charlotte on the side of my marriage. She was labeled a homewrecker and other disturbing names I'd rather forget. My Charlotte deserved none of the backlash she endured.

In the end, I was the married man who broke my vows.

No one held a gun to my head. My actions were because I fell in love with my sister's best friend, and no one in the world could stop me.

Until they did.

The resentment toward my family ran deep. My father's actions came as no surprise. He wanted to protect our family's reputation.

My mother, however, let me down. A woman I'd always highly respected treated Charlotte like she was nothing.

At the time of our affair, I'd never once imagined myself if the roles were reversed aside from prom when Charlotte took what's-his-face as her date. In the end, I won the battle and owned her on her classroom desk.

But there are no winners in the game of love. Not when there's more than one person involved.

Charlotte's trust in me dwindled the longer we snuck around. Our fights became more frequent, and the small amount of time we were together was me trying to justify how she had no reason to think I was fucking a woman who may be my wife but was completely dead to me.

Then, the roles reversed, and I was forced to watch her with another man. My thoughts were deadly. Just how much I wanted to get rid of Baker was undeniable. I'd spent every night wondering if he was touching her, driving myself to the brink of insanity until my actions became forceful and necessary.

Was it wrong for me to touch her when she committed to another man?

I needed her

End of fucking story.

It was not enough to think love would get us through this. In ways, we were toxic for each other. Our past threatened our future. No matter how much we tried, there was no escaping the damage which was done.

After the months when both our lives turned upside down for the second time, a rainbow presented itself after the storm.

Charlotte is carrying my baby.

The chains of our past finally broke last night when Charlotte came forward with the truth. Eight years ago, Charlotte gave birth to our stillborn son and buried him without me knowing.

Hearing this revelation was hard to endure. My mistakes were even greater than I could have ever imagined. Had I known at the time, I would have left Samantha to care for Charlotte and our baby. Sure, our families would have disowned us, but it wouldn't have mattered if we had each other.

The moon filters inside the room as I stare at Charlotte sleeping beside me. Her skin is glowing, the signs of an expectant mother. She looks peaceful and content. Despite my need to own her again, her rest is more important.

Eventually, I fall asleep until the daylight shines through the window. The sun is barely peeking behind the clouds, a typical winter's day. Charlotte stirs beside me before turning to place her hand on my bare chest.

"Good morning," I whisper.

ɾ eyes slowly flutter open. "You're here."

I kiss her hand. "Where else would I be?"

Charlotte's eyes remain closed, but a smile spreads across her face before she turns herself around completely and places my arm over her, smothered by my embrace. With her ass pressed against my cock, she's not playing fair right now.

My hands move to her tits, squeezing them with a desperate need to fuck her sweet pussy right now. I kiss the top of her shoulder, knowing I can't wait any longer and slide myself in. Her moans are sounds of heaven. Her tight walls trap my cock inside and tease me with the need to blow straight away, but I control myself, taking it slow and savoring every moment.

Charlotte reaches back as the bedsheet falls and exposes her tits.

"Hmmm. I'm about to ..." She doesn't finish the sentence as her entire body clenches in my grip. At the same time, I push hard, expelling my own blissful finish.

"Is this how I should expect to wake up every day?"

"I'm greedy and always get what I want," I remind her.

"Lex Edwards greedy? I would never have thought so," she teases before her stomach growls. "Great, baby is hungry."

"How about I order some food so the baby doesn't starve?"

"Sure, bring it all. The baby wants everything."

I lean over and grab the room service menu while Charlotte uses the bathroom. Not wanting to leave anything out, I dial the number and order several dishes and coffee for myself.

She walks out, still naked, and climbs back into bed as I

use the bathroom to brush my teeth and place my robe on to be able to answer the door.

"You know you can't be naked if room service arrives," I inform her sternly.

Charlotte throws the sheets off her, spreading her legs on the bed while moving her hand between them. Slowly, she rubs her clit as a groan rumbles inside my throat from the sight of her being naughty. *This woman will be the death of me.*

"They'll be here any minute," I warn her.

She ignores me, continuing to pleasure herself which is driving me crazy. Then, she slides her fingers inside as her back arches against the soft white pillows.

I cross my arms beneath my chest, trying to remain strong, but I'm a man with needs, and right now, I need to be between her legs.

My hands hastily untie the knot on the robe before removing it entirely. Then, I dive into the bed and lash my tongue into her pussy like it's my last meal on Earth. Charlotte grabs my hair, begging me not to stop until she can't control herself, and her body shudders in delight.

A knock on the door comes just after, forcing me to pull away and place my robe back on swiftly. I wait for Charlotte to get under the covers, which she does with a grin on her face.

When she's covered entirely, I lick my lips to taste the remnants of her cum, followed by a smirk.

"Sweet."

Charlotte laughs softly as I open the door to a young woman with bright red cheeks. Surely, she heard us and can probably put two and two together hence why she's looking very embarrassed right now.

"Room service," she stammers, unable to make eye contact with me.

"Thank you," I respond, signing the bill. "How about I take it inside myself? My wife isn't feeling well."

"I'm sorry to hear that," she responds politely, still diverting her eyes. "If there's anything you need, please don't hesitate to contact the front desk."

"I'm sure I can take care of her just the way she needs."

I take the tray from her hands and close the door as Charlotte bursts out laughing. "The poor girl. You made it so awkward for her."

"How did I do that?"

"For starters, you're a very hot man, and you answer the door wearing a robe with my cum all over your face."

I place the tray next to Charlotte. "Excuse me, I licked the cum off you, so trust me when I say there wasn't a single drop left."

Charlotte shuffles over as I sit beside her while she tries to hide her smile. The aroma of pancakes airs in the room after she lifts the lid and pours maple syrup all over them. I wasn't sure how much to order, but she appears satisfied with the stack of three with sausage and eggs on the side.

"You're such a gentleman. The perfect catch since there's a lot of men who would not do that."

With the coffee cup in my hand, I take a long sip before her comment sinks in. "And how do you know that?"

Charlotte's eyes widen. "From friends."

My lips press together. "Nice lie. Please continue to lie to me about how you remained celibate while we were apart."

Charlotte snorts rudely, making it very clear she's annoyed. "Did you remain celibate while we were apart?"

"I'm a man. It's different."

She places her fork down, narrowing her eyes with a pinched expression. "So, it's okay for you to fuck a million women, but I was supposed to pine for you?"

"A million is being dramatic," I drag.

Charlotte digs her fork into her pancakes in silence, but then I remember I need to be sympathetic since she's carrying my kid. Now is not the time to be a possessive dickhead.

I place my coffee down, then turn to face her. "Whether it was one or a million, no other woman could ever replace you. If I didn't make the mistake of leaving you, I would have lived a very happy life with you by my side."

Her shoulders relax. "I'm sorry. It must be the hormones."

Even though I know she needs to eat, I move the tray away and climb on top without trying to squash her, mindful of my weight over her petite body.

"Our little fight has caused a problem," I murmur, sucking on her nipples as she moans.

"Oh, what's that?"

I lift my eyes to meet hers. "I need to own you, right now. Again."

She runs her finger across my bottom lip.

"*Fuck me!*" she breathes.

Time is of the essence. I don't allow for any words, sliding myself in while kissing her the entire time. She tastes like maple syrup, sweet and addictive. Her nails scratch down my back as I warn her I'm going to blow first. My body begins to convulse, my groans expelling until she follows in her own orgasmic finish.

"That was ..." She chokes, then catches her breath. "How is it possible you've made me come three times in less than an hour?"

I kiss her lips before climbing off, then arrange the food back so she can eat.

"Finish your meal, and I'll show you how we can top that record and hit four times."

Her lips curve upward into a smile as she eats with ease but scolds me for the lack of coffee.

"I can't believe we're here."

I nod with a grin. "Me neither."

"And we're married."

"We sure are."

"And having a baby..."

I take a moment to think about it all. How second chances are a rarity, and everything I've ever wanted is sitting on this bed beside me.

"Mrs. Edwards," I say with a bated breath. "It's only the beginning."

Charlotte kisses my hand and then finishes her meal. It's almost time to leave, and just as I'm about to bury myself in her again, the knock on the door is the biggest cock-blocker known to man. I know the knock very well. I heard it every single day as a child growing up in a house with the most impatient sister.

"Adriana, fuck off," I yell.

Charlotte pushes my chest slightly. "You know she has a key, right?"

"And?"

"I don't want the whole world to see me naked."

"It's just Adriana. I'm sure she's seen you naked before."

"Yeah, but it was junior high, and it was more like a 'count to three and lift your top up' so we can compare breast sizes."

My brows draw in. "You really did that?"

"Yes. Didn't guys do that in high school, like in urinals?'

I shake my head at the thought. "No, to answer the question. I do not look at other guys' dicks to compare."

Charlotte grins. "Maybe because you've got no competition, baby."

The sound of the swipe card echoes then the door opens. It's not only Adriana but Elijah, Kate and Eric too.

Jesus fucking Christ, why is Eric looking at me all weird and stalker-like.

"Seriously, get the fuck out," I warn them before burying my head back into Charlotte's neck, hoping it's too much for them and they'll leave promptly.

"As much as I love you, big brother, you have to get your naked ass out of here. The inn booked a traveling polka group, and unless you want to have polka tunes stuck in your head all week, it's time to leave."

"How long do we have?" I ask in annoyance.

"Fifteen minutes, at most," Adriana responds after a quick glance at the clock.

"Then get the hell out of here and let me enjoy my woman for five minutes," I bark, climbing on top of Charlotte as she giggles under the sheets.

"Okay, that's my cue to leave... see ya outside." Adriana waves.

"Five minutes? Really, Lex, is that all it takes?" Elijah teases.

"Okay, you two peeping Toms, let's get out of here." Kate grabs Eric and Elijah's arms, shutting the door behind her.

I kiss Charlotte's lips, then pull away. "Did you hear that? Fifteen minutes. What can I do in fifteen minutes?"

"Hmm," Charlotte murmurs with her eyes dancing. "Maybe you can lie on your back, and I can get on my knees and suck this beautiful cock of yours until you cum and decorate my chest with a beautiful pearl necklace."

She only had to say the word *suck* to make me rock hard.

I shuffle so I'm on my back with my arm resting behind my head, eager to watch her suck me off. Charlotte gets on her knees, then lowers her mouth to tease me. My whole body waits in anticipation until her mouth wraps around the tip, and she takes me all in.

A deep rumbling growl escapes me while watching the woman I love giving me the best fucking head of my life.

So good, I give her the prettiest pearl necklace in return.

TEN

The time we brought Amelia home

My mother once told me the birth of your first child will always hold a special place in your heart. It's a life-changing moment where time stands still the second your firstborn child is laid in your arms.

There is an overwhelming sense of love, and everything you thought you once knew about life makes no sense at all before this very moment.

It was four days ago when Charlotte brought Amelia into this world. Nothing has ever felt this perfect. This tiny human being had a hold over me, and my desire to protect her kicked into stealth mode the second her little lungs let out a cry because she was finally here.

The call from Charlotte to say her water broke, to the rush to the hospital to give birth, all of it was a giant blur. The sheer panic from the possibility of something going wrong never dissipated. My knowledge and experience in medicine made it even more stressful. I'd seen worst-case scenarios, which perhaps was why I hovered around the medical staff to ensure they were following protocol.

We finally made it here, the end of our hospital journey, and ready for our new life as a family of three.

The ride home from the hospital is incredibly slow on my part. I chose to drive, not wanting a driver to be in control of the wheel. Charlotte comments on my speed but decides to ignore the obnoxious horns, impatiently telling me to move faster. They can all fuck right off. My daughter needs to make it safely home. That's all I care about.

The car is parked in the garage underneath the building. With the carrier unfastened and in my hands, I carry Amelia with one arm and insist Charlotte hold onto my other arm for support. Given the cesarean, she's still sore but able to walk at a slow pace.

Amelia continues to sleep like an angel while we enter the apartment. At the same time, Charlotte lets out a long-winded yawn. It's been a tough few days on her body, and I'm worried she's not getting enough rest since Amelia enjoys staying awake during the night. A hard lesson we have learned in the short time she's been with us.

"Why don't you head to bed?" My hand reaches out to cup her chin gently, hoping she'll listen and not be stubborn as usual. "You need rest."

Charlotte lets out another yawn. "But what if she wakes up?"

"Then I'll take care of her."

"But what if she needs a feed?"

She has a point. Charlotte isn't producing enough milk yet to be able to pump copious amounts in advance.

"Okay, so why don't we try pumping again before you sleep?" I openly suggest. "Your milk should come in real soon."

With a barely-there nod, Charlotte decides to take a shower first to rid herself of the hospital smell, as she calls it. I use the time wisely, preparing the pump and getting the bed comfortable for Charlotte. Her shower takes too long, so I check to make sure she hasn't fallen asleep in there.

When she's ready to finish, I help her out carefully so Charlotte doesn't fall since she still has a bandage on her stomach. Also, her limbs and muscles are still weak.

"We need to change the bandage tomorrow," I inform her.

"Yes, Dr. Edwards," she manages with a soft chuckle, then winces in pain. "Karma, for teasing you."

We move to the bedroom, where Charlotte changes with my help. I've transferred Amelia to her cradle to sleep, worried she's cramped in her carrier. Thankfully, she continues to sleep since Charlotte is on the verge of passing out.

I take the breast pump out, latching it on carefully to see if Charlotte releases some milk. A few drops come out, then a few more, enough for one feed for Amelia. When it's clear nothing else comes out, Charlotte throws her head back on the pillow and begins to cry.

"I'm a failure."

Quickly, I put the lid on the bottle and placed it on the nightstand, removing the suction carefully from her breasts.

"You're not a failure. You're a mother who just gave birth to her first child."

"It's not my first child," she mumbles.

I let out a sigh, forgetting Charlotte's trauma which is still weighing heavy on her mind as it does on mine. The difference is that I didn't give birth to a stillborn baby, nor was I there to experience the trauma firsthand.

Softly, I grab Charlotte's hand and kiss it gently. "I'm

here. I will always be here. Please let me help you. Amelia is our child, and I don't want you to ever think you're in this alone, but you need to talk to me, baby. I know you're scared and tired and think about Alexander all the time."

"I keep thinking, what-if?" She begins to speak with a choke in her voice. "What if I did have him? Would I have ever told you?"

There's no answer I'm able to give. How can I imagine the 'what-if' when everything I want is inside this very room?

"I don't know, Charlotte."

"Honestly, I wouldn't have," she says with conviction. "I would have forever thought you chose your wife and child with her at the time over me. I never wanted us to be second."

I take a deep breath, entertaining her thoughts for just a moment. "You would never have been second. I promise you that."

"I go over it in my head. More so in the last few weeks as we drew closer to giving birth. Would I have studied Law? Would I have gone back home to my dad? What if—"

"Charlotte," I interrupt calmly. "You need to stop asking yourself these questions. There is no answer. I'm here, and I promise you that if I knew you were having our baby, I would have been there for you."

"But you wouldn't have left her," she insists.

I'm not sure if it's the hormones talking or if I should accept her feelings about our past.

"I left the moment I found out the child she carried belonged to someone else. Did I stay with her when I thought it was my child? Yes, because I thought it was the right thing to do. God, Charlotte, I was in over my head. I wasn't innocent in all this, and neither was Samantha. But we can't keep going over this expecting a different outcome."

"I know there's no different outcome," she mumbles while twitching her fingers. "Look, I'm tired."

"Then please get some rest. I will wake you if I need you."

"Promise?"

"I promise."

I leave the room to quickly shower so Amelia doesn't wake up. Dressed in my sweats and tee, I'm expecting a sleepless night once Amelia finds her lungs. I sit beside my sleeping wife and quickly answer some emails on my phone before Amelia begins to stir.

It always starts with a cute baby noise until it blows out into a wail. My feet touch the ground as I get out of bed and take Amelia out, bringing her to the changing table for a quick diaper change, to which she almost cries. Her face does this scrunch, then her lips begin to quiver, but then she relaxes.

When she's in a fresh diaper, I grab the bottle to feed her. Only remembering now it's cold, I carry Amelia in my arms to the kitchen. Carefully, I managed with one hand to boil some water on the stovetop to sit the bottle in for a few minutes. I rock Amelia back and forth until the bottle is warm and begin to feed her. She manages to drink the entire bottle. Then, I burp her until she falls into another sleep.

Once it's evident she's out again, I turn the lamp off and place Amelia in her cradle before settling back into bed. Maybe this isn't so hard. So, I wake up once at night. It's not like I was used to sleeping before this. I've always been a night owl.

With darkness once again casting over the room, my

ɔ drop, only realizing now how exhausting the
. days have also been for me.

It's pitch black when Charlotte's voice wakes me.

"Lex," she whispers, touching my arm gently.

My eyes spring open in a panic. "What's wrong?"

In a daze, I go to turn the lamp on, almost blinding myself, then rub my face to wake myself up. My ears listen out for Amelia, but she's quiet. What the hell is wrong then?

"My milk came in."

I turn to look over and see Charlotte's tank completely drenched.

A relaxed smile falls upon my face. "What a relief."

My body twists to help her remove the wet tank and bra beneath it. When she's completely bare-chested, I try not to focus on everything engorged. The veins surrounding her nipples are blue and prominent. Her nipples appear much larger.

Listen, control yourself. This isn't the time to get turned out by your wife's tits even though your dick is now hard, and there's no fucking stopping it.

"It's okay. You can admit they look weird."

I hop out of bed and open the drawer, grabbing a new bra and shirt. "They don't look weird. They look perfectly normal for a lactating mother."

"You think I look disgusting. It's why you can't even look at them."

Motioning for her to extend her arms, I slide a new bra on and then help her with the shirt.

"Quite the opposite, they're quiet, umm... how shall I say it?"

"Just say it," Charlotte blurts in annoyance. "Hideous."

"Sexy."

"Sexy?" Charlotte glances down, furrowing her brows in confusion. "These things?"

"Yes, so if we can please stop talking about it, I would appreciate it."

I toss Charlotte's wet clothes into the hamper while Amelia cries. Lifting her from the cradle, I take soft steps and bring her back to our bed. Charlotte takes her from my arms, then attempts to latch her on, to which Amelia finally begins to suck.

"Thank God," Charlotte says, then winces. "Ow."

"Just breathe," I tell her, rubbing her shoulder to distract her, knowing it's painful for women when their milk finally comes in.

I never imagined watching my child with the woman I love.

But here we are.

It's such a beautiful sight.

"Just perfect," I whisper.

Charlotte relaxes her shoulders with an adoring smile. "Our family. I couldn't have asked for anything more perfect."

ELEVEN

The time a life began and one ended

Some say death may be the greatest of human blessings.

I never truly understood this until the reality faced our family brutally just a few short months ago.

Elijah is and has been—suffering.

The hardest part has been watching him deteriorate and losing my sister with him.

Every night has become sleepless, praying for a miracle to cure him and the endless worrying over Adriana's well-being and the life of their unborn child.

That was until Andrew Elijah Evans entered the world just a few minutes ago.

Elijah sits beside Adriana, holding her hand with his fragile one. His prominent bones make it understandably difficult to find the strength to carry his son, but it's important he do so.

"Elijah, are you ready to hold your son?" Mom asks,

cradling baby Andrew in her hands like the proud grand-mother she is.

With a weak smile, Elijah nods without a word before Mom gently places a wrapped Andrew into his arms.

Mom hovers, worried he'll drop him given his frail state, but I watch on, knowing this moment will stay with me forever. The moment I held Amelia, I envisioned our future. All those milestones from the first birthday to the first time she'll get into the driver's seat and start the engine. It brought me so much joy, knowing our lives will be filled with so much love and it's only just begun.

Yet, in front of me, a life is about to end.

I shake my head, trying to clear my morbid thoughts, then reach out to touch my sister's hand. Adriana rests her head against the pillow, silently gazing at Elijah. The birth was long, and of course, she's utterly exhausted. I continue to hold her hand to reassure her it'll be okay.

But I know it won't be.

"Lex," Adriana's voice cracks as she speaks. "Please take him away from Elijah."

"Are you sure?"

"He's tired," is all she says.

I release Adriana's hand from mine, then move around the bed to where Elijah sits. Carefully, I lift Andrew from his arms to see a sigh of relief from Elijah. Mom glances at me with a knowing stare and then offers Elijah something to eat or drink. Gently, I place Andrew in his plastic crib supplied by the hospital.

My father walks into the room after speaking to the midwife and ensuring all is well. The moment his eyes lay on Elijah, he draws his brows together, then his gaze flicks to me.

"Adriana, sweetheart. How are you feeling?" Dad asks, kissing her forehead.

"Tired," she barely manages.

"How about you get some rest? I'm sure Elijah could use the rest too."

Adriana nods, not arguing like she usually would.

"Do you want me to help you, Dad?"

"It's okay, son. Your mother and I will make sure Elijah is settled. You stay with your sister."

It takes both my parents to help Elijah up and transfer him to the wheelchair. His limbs are so frail, making it difficult for him to walk long distances. The reality of his deterioration is so visual, making every moment in his presence so incredibly difficult to process.

Adriana reaches out her hand to touch Elijah, but neither of them says a word. Moments later, Dad wheels him out, leaving me alone with my sister.

"So, how do you really feel?" I ask, knowing she's trying to put on a brave face for my parents.

"Like I've made a mistake bringing a child into this world without a father."

A heavy sigh escapes me, and I sit on the plastic chair and move closer to her.

"I'm here. I'll always be here to help you."

"You have your own family, Lex."

My hand reaches out for hers, then I squeeze it tight. "I will not allow you to raise him alone, you understand me? He's my nephew."

Adriana turns her head in the opposite direction, glancing at the window.

"I can't do this," she chokes, the stammer in her words communicating her pain. "I'm going to lose him."

My anger grows every second I see my sister in pain. The tightness in my chest refuses to dissipate even as I try to take breaths. All of this is unfair, but so much of my thoughts circle back to Elijah and his refusal of treatment. Maybe, if I pushed harder, he would have agreed and given himself a longer chance at life.

The guilt weighs heavily on my mind. Should I have done more? Battling with a man who is sick of fighting is perhaps the most brutal battle of all. Elijah is exhausted. His suffering is nothing any of us can imagine.

But my biggest worry is now my sister.

I cannot lose her.

There's a gentle knock on the door.

"Come in," I say.

The door opens as Charlotte walks in, pushing the stroller. With a forced smile, I know her too well to understand she's terrified of what is about to come. We've talked about this openly and how useless we feel given everything is out of our control.

"Are you up for visitors?" Charlotte questions with slight hesitation.

"You're family," Adriana mumbles.

Charlotte walks in my direction, planting a kiss on my lips before moving toward Andrew. I'm distracted by my daughter being in my presence, admiring her sleeping peacefully inside her stroller.

"Adriana," Charlotte whispers with a proud smile. "He's beautiful. Can I hold him?"

"Of course."

When it comes to babies, Charlotte is a natural. She picks him up so effortlessly, talking softly while cradling him in her arms.

"He has the Edwards' nose," Charlotte mentions with ease, "and Elijah's light hair."

"I'll have to look at him every day, and it will remind me Elijah is no longer here," Adriana blurts out.

My eyes dart to Charlotte, her painful expression struggling to compose her emotions.

"Adriana," Charlotte begins until my sister shakes her head.

"No, Charlie. Why is no one talking about the fact that my husband will be dead soon, and I'll be all alone raising a son who will look just like him."

I clear my throat, aware Charlotte is just about to break down and cry again.

"Adriana," I say softly. "We need to focus on now. Elijah is still with us. Let him enjoy his family. These memories are priceless."

Adriana turns to look at me, but her face says it all—she's done fighting. Her pale skin and tired eyes worry me. Even though she has just given birth, I'm unable to see the parental love kick in with her son. Not the way I saw Charlotte's face light up the moment Amelia came roaring into this world.

"I want to be alone now," is all she says with a blank stare.

"Of course." I kiss her on the forehead as Charlotte begins to place Andrew back in the crib.

"Take Andy with you."

"Andy?" Charlotte tilts her head, then shakes her head with a small smile. "It's a cute nickname. But are you sure you don't want to have some alone time with him?"

"No," Adriana insists. "I want to be alone."

Charlotte nods then places the newly named Andy

down in the crib. She pushes him out as I push Amelia's stroller, but I stop just shy of the door. "We'll be outside if you need us."

Adriana turns her back, facing the window again without another word.

As the door closes behind me, Charlotte drops her head to where Andy sleeps quietly.

"Lex, I'm worried."

My hand reaches out as I pull her into me. The moment her head touches my chest, she begins to cry. I kiss her forehead, trying to comfort her.

"I'm worried too."

Charlotte pulls away. "Post-natal depression is hard enough to manage on its own. You throw in losing your husband, and I can't begin to imagine the pain she's in. Adriana needs help and someone with her at all times. Maybe we can do a roster system to help?"

"Mom is already on it," I inform her gently. "We will do what we need to do. Time is running out."

And with those words out in the open, we both know it is the hard cold truth.

The sound is loud, like a tornado siren warning everyone of destruction.

It sends chills throughout me, even though I've heard it many times during my hospital internship.

A life is just about to end.

Any ounce of hope any of us had, a miracle of some sort, is fading like the light in his eyes. The once blue orbs have long faded into darkness, making this all the more real.

We stand together inside the room, my mother beside me as she tries to remain strong for my sister. Across from us, my father holds onto Adriana knowing our time with Elijah is almost at an end, but she chooses to hover near the door.

Doctor Brady places his hand on Adriana's arm. "Mrs. Evans, I think it's time you said goodbye to your husband."

I'm unable to fight back the tears, watching my sister's blank expression as if she's on autopilot and numb to the pain. My father is struggling, emotions overcoming him in a way I've never seen before. Even at his own father's funeral, my father remained composed.

But this is unfair.

He's too young.

A sob escapes my mother, forcing me to place my arm around her shoulder to console her while she rocks Andy back and forth in an attempt to shield him from the grief surrounding us.

Then, Dr. Brady glances at me, reminding me of what he just asked Adriana to do.

Without a second thought, I move to my sister, urging her to say goodbye. Each step we take closer to Elijah brings a new pain I never knew could exist.

Elijah is lying in bed, unable to open his eyes any longer. He's pale and gaunt with his skin almost gray. The remaining strands of his once-luscious locks are barely visible. But the hardest thing to see is the shade of blue spreading across his lips.

A croak expels from his mouth as he attempts to lift his hand to touch his wife. With no strength left to fight, he drops his hand, defeated.

With a strained voice, he mutters his final words, "I did

this for us. You deserve a life with someone who will see it through with you till the very end. Don't hate me, Adriana... please..."

The staff rushes around in one last attempt to save him. No matter the situation, there is always the possibility of a medical miracle until the sound of a flat line echoes in the room, just as it does now.

Dr. Brady looks at the nurse, shaking his head slowly. The staff remove their masks before Dr. Brady glances at the clock.

"Time of death... 11:53 p.m."

My mother's sobs are the loudest in the room, and a nurse rushes to her side to help with Andy as my mother struggles to stand. My father stands in shock, his face stripped of any hope he had left in him.

Instinctively, I wrap my arms around my sister, needing to protect her from the pain. I hold her close to me, desperately wanting to feel the beat of her heart against my chest. I need her to remain breathing, afraid if her heart breaks into a million pieces, she will take this journey with him.

Unable to fight my emotions, tears fall down my cheeks as I hold onto her for as long as possible. Around us, the staff begins the procedure by covering him with a blanket.

Adriana is still in my arms, with not a single sound and barely a breath. I squeeze her tighter, but then her body begins to shudder like she's standing outside in the dead of winter blanketed with cold.

Then, she buries her head into my chest and lets out a startling scream. The pain in her cry ricochets like a bullet inside a small metal room. The sound is forever engrained in my memory. It's the sound of losing your husband.

Your best friend.

The father of your only child.

My embrace is tight, but I don't want to let her go until my parents take her from my arms and try to console her.

It all becomes a blur, the pain and grief not allowing us to breathe normally. My sister continues to sob into my father's chest as I walk out to a corridor of people waiting for news.

They didn't have to wait. They heard my sister.

Charlotte is being comforted by Eric as they both sob in each other's arms. Charlotte lets go and rushes to where I stand, burying her head into my chest and holding onto me as if her life depends on it.

Rocky and Nikki are standing beside Eric. They do their best to hold it back, but like all of us, grief is a force to be reckoned with.

Kate is sitting beside the stroller with Amelia sleeping inside. Her head is lowered, unable to make eye contact, but the tears fall onto her lap while she sits in silence.

"Lex," Charlotte calls in thin and strained sobs. "Andy..."

"He's inside."

"I want to be with Adriana."

I nod, then glance over at Kate. She lifts her head, her bloodshot eyes meeting mine with a pained stare.

"I'll stay with Amelia. Take your time."

With my heart beating incredibly fast, I open the door, scared of what I'll find inside.

Adriana is still in my father's embrace, barely able to hold herself up, and my mother helps to make sure she doesn't collapse. The nurse is still with Andy, allowing our family a moment to come to terms with losing Elijah.

As Charlotte enters the room behind me, her gaze darts to the covered body on the bed, then onto my sister.

Charlotte runs to Adriana, ripping her away from my father as Adriana begins to sob into Charlotte's shoulder.

"He's gone," she screams. *"My husband is gone."*

And just like that, Elijah Jean Evans left this world and finally became free of the pain his body endured.

As for the rest of us, our nightmare is only beginning.

TWELVE

The time when wounds began to heal

The day we lost Elijah, a piece of each one of us died with him.

My brother was finally laid to rest.

Grief is the price we pay for loving someone so deeply. The pain is immeasurable, and like waves in the ocean, it comes and goes, some days greater than others.

There are moments when we're able to take a step forward. Unfortunately, though, most of the time, the grief suffocates any hope of a bright future again.

The last few months have been the hardest I've ever endured. I'd pushed away my wife for fear of losing her. None of it made sense how loving someone can hurt so much. How losing them is our biggest fear. The misery I'd inflicted on Charlotte was unforgivable and out of character, given on our wedding day I'd promised her nothing would ever tear us apart again.

It got to a point where my mistakes became my identity

like I had some evil twin dictating my every move, out to destroy everything.

The reality, once again, was the wake-up call I desperately needed. There was no way I was going to lose Charlotte to *him*. Seeing Baker on the dance floor brought all my mistakes to the surface. He held my wife in his arms, and for every second that passed, inside of me shattered like broken glass.

The way she looked at him ripped open my old wounds, the pain just simply unbearable.

Charlotte Edwards is the air I breathe.

Without her—I am *dead*.

Forgiveness is not as simple as I'd hoped for. The last few days tested both of us.

Being in the same house and not sleeping in bed together was incredibly hard. Every time we managed to be in the same room, I ached to reach out and caress her.

It's her smile, her laughter, and the way she tells some ridiculous story about Eric which always ended up boring me since the man has the most unfortunate luck. All of it was a piece of her I'd taken advantage of, never realizing how important the simple things are until they're taken away from you.

We were back on talking terms, but I knew she was still processing everything. The woman is stubborn at the best of times. Charlotte made it perfectly clear she wasn't ready for me to touch her intimately, despite my selfish need to take her in the parking lot the night of the event.

I'm clinging to hope we can somehow get through this. We'd been through so much already, and our love for each other tested many times. Yet, what doesn't kill you supposedly makes you stronger.

My hope and my prayers were answered thirty minutes

ago when Charlotte busted into the boardroom and requested to see me in private.

"What's wrong?" I asked, panicked.

She buried her head in my chest while sobbing loudly.

"I love you," she cried. "It hurts, but I love you."

"If I have to spend my entire life earning your forgiveness, I will do just that. I can't … we can't be apart. I cannot let you go."

"I don't want you to let me go. We promised it was ride or die. I'm standing here, breathing, alive, and want to give our family a second chance to become one again."

The Bluetooth inside the car begins to ring as I drive down the freeway toward home. Adriana's name flashes on the screen, so I answer in case something is wrong since she has Amelia.

"Adriana," I answer, rushed. "What's wrong?"

"Nothing's wrong, Lex. I'm sitting outside with Andy and Amelia. They're in the sandpit playing."

My shoulders immediately relax. "Okay, just making sure."

"So, how are things at home? I spoke to Charlie."

"If you spoke to Charlotte, then you know…"

"I'm sorry, Lex."

"What are you sorry for?"

"I just feel responsible for your marriage almost ending," she admits with a heaviness in her tone. "I mean, my husband is the reason why you could have lost everything."

I shake my head even though she's unable to see. The

last thing Adriana needs to do is blame herself for another thing.

"I'm the idiot who screwed up my marriage. Don't blame yourself. I've made some really bad decisions, and if anyone should be saying sorry, it's me."

Adriana's cumbersome sigh echoes through the speaker. "When is it supposed to get easier?"

There isn't an answer I can give her, despite wanting to protect my sister.

"I don't know. But it's Eric's birthday this weekend, and Rocky is flying over again. You know what happens when Rocky has had too much to drink, and Eric is oversensitive about his age."

"There's always something to look forward to, I guess." Adriana chuckles softly. "Anyway, I called you to ask if it was okay if Amelia stayed the night?"

"I guess, but are you sure?"

"Yeah, she keeps Andy entertained, plus I figured since you and Charlie have made up, you'll be busy in the bedroom."

This time, it's my turn to laugh. "My wife is hot."

"She sure is," Adriana muses. "Lucky Julian didn't sweep her off her feet."

My jaw clenches at the thought of him having any claim to my wife. Then, with a slight growl, my foot pushes down on the accelerator to speed up to the exit.

"Adriana," I warn. "Don't start."

"C'mon, Lex. He's gone now. You've proven your point, and it's over for him. I'm sure he will eventually move on and find someone else."

"Can we please stop discussing him?"

"Fine," Adriana drags. "Before you ravage your wife, are you sure you're still free to come to the daycare with me on

Friday? I just know I'll get emotional leaving Andy for the first time, and someone needs to make sure I don't chicken out."

"I'll be there," I assure her. "Bye, Adriana."

"Bye, horndog."

My lips curve upward at her last comment, unable to hold back my smile as the gates to our house open.

When we first purchased the house a few months ago, it was the right decision, given we hadn't known how sick Elijah was. Charlotte missed Manhattan, but we both agreed to raise our family in LA. The thing I love most about our house is the space for us to grow. It has everything we want, including a large yard with views of the canyons.

I park my car in the usual spot, then take a moment to compose myself. Adriana's mention of Baker has me rattled yet again. I'm a jealous man, something I'm not ashamed of. Though more often than not, my jealousy becomes dangerous, and my thoughts become misplaced.

Yeah, I would have killed him with my bare hands if jail time wasn't a possibility.

My key jiggles in the lock, finally unlocking the back door. Immediately, my eyes fall upon Charlotte, leaning against the countertop. She's still dressed in the gray skirt she wore earlier and a white blouse showing just enough cleavage to not draw attention. Her black pumps are my favorite. My eyes wander to her lean legs as I bite my lip to control my urges.

Inside my chest, my heartbeat quickens, making my breathing ragged and uneven. I slow down my movements, admiring my beautiful wife, who accepts me for all my flaws and mistakes, and chooses to build a life with me.

Her big brown eyes glance up with a smile gracing her pink lips.

"Lex," she breathes, taking me all in as I place my keys on the counter.

We need to say so many words to each other, but perhaps, for now, no more words are left to be said. Each step closer to her, I grow hot and feverish, my body hyper-aware of her presence.

The desperate need to be inside her is all I can think about. Yet, unlike the other night when I was ruthless with my intentions, Charlotte's inviting gaze explores my body as she unknowingly bites the corner of her lip.

I'm not proud of fucking Charlotte against the car and degrading her because of my own insecurities. Anyone could have seen us and more disturbingly, seen my wife being fucked. There are sick and twisted people in this world with nothing surprising me anymore.

Although she never stopped or pushed me away, and her body relaxed when I blew inside her, I should have known better.

The connection, and love, are more than just sex.

My hands reach out, cupping her face as my mouth finds hers. Her lips taste warm and sweet, as does the moan that escapes during our kiss. I take my time, gentle with my tongue, desperate to savor this moment despite my urges threatening to turn me into a beast again. Sure, I can turn her around and fuck her pussy in a matter of seconds.

But I need more.

I need to *own* her.

Charlotte places her hands on my chest, taking a deep breath. "I know what you need, baby."

Her deep and prolonged stare sends a pleasurable ache all over my body. I reach out to play with a lock of her hair.

"I need to own you," I murmur. "You know what you need to do."

Charlotte's hands wander down my chest and stop at my belt. Slowly, she fiddles with the buckle, keeping her eyes on me with a teasing stare. Her fingers pull the zipper down. Then she yanks my boxers down without hesitation as my cock springs free.

The sound of her breath expelling drives me insane. I'm fucking rock hard and could blow by just continuing to watch the desire etched on her face.

Her mouth forms a circle, opening the gap with her eyes fixating on me. The tip of her tongue teases against her lips as she moves forward to take me in.

My body jerks forward, a grunt echoing inside our kitchen as my fists clench into a ball and rest against the marble countertop.

The inside of her mouth is warm like a blanket on a cold winter's night. Charlotte takes her time, sliding me in and out, forcing me to control my need to blow at this very second.

Charlotte has memorized every single part of my body and each inch of my throbbing cock. My eyes are focused on the saliva building up around her mouth. The more, the fucking merrier. When her gaze flicks up, the submissive stare is enough for me to take what I want.

She knows just the man I am and exactly what will get me off to a roaring finish.

My hands rest on the back of her head, and without a care in the world, I thrust myself in deep, desperate to hear my cock hitting the back of her throat.

Her eyes widen as she makes a choking sound, the sound heightening my senses to the point of madness. Unable to control myself, I hold her head in position until her eyes begin to water then I release her abruptly.

"Again," she begs with pleading eyes.

This time, I run my hands through her hair, forcefully pushing her deep until her choke echoes louder. My wife is fucking beautiful when she takes me all in, submissive to my commands when I need to own her.

My muscles tense as my entire body succumbs to my desires. The beat of my heart is racing a marathon while the hairs on my arms and the nape of my neck rise.

"One more," I command.

Charlotte opens her mouth wide again, staring back with a watery gaze. I thrust hard. Then all my nerve endings hit their peak as I blow inside her mouth.

I let out a drawn-out growl, unable to control the warmth all over my body.

"Fuck," I grit with a ragged breath.

Charlotte throws her head back, almost hitting the countertop. Her chest rises and falls as she tries to catch her own breath.

But we are far from finished.

"So, Mrs. Edwards, do you have plans for me?"

A slow smile builds on Charlotte's face as she licks around the edge of her lips, making sure she's tasted all of me. Then, she presses her palms against the marble countertop and raises her body to sit on top of it.

"I know you're hungry, and I've got something you can feast on," she teases, spreading her legs apart.

Through the sheer lace panties, my eyes focus on the moist fabric. *Fuck, she's soaking wet, and I am hungry.*

"Famished," I inform her.

Her hand moves between her legs then she shoves her panties aside, exposing her delicious pussy. With her other hand, she clutches my hair and shoves my face right into her.

"Then, eat me," she demands.

THIRTEEN

The time when tragedy brought us a blessing

Why won't she pick up her fucking phone?

The memories plague me like a reoccurring nightmare.

I could have lost my wife and baby.

All because of *him*.

Falling pregnant with another baby wasn't in our plans, though—a blessing in disguise. Charlotte was shocked when I told her at Christmas, in our bathroom while our family was celebrating inside our living room.

I'd memorized every inch of Charlotte's body. The way her tits sat so firmly against her chest to the size of her nipples. I've spent hours devouring her body because I couldn't get enough.

Then, there was this glow. The rose in her cheeks. There were simple things she hadn't realized she'd been doing. Charlotte thrives on routine and is consistent. For example, she enjoys fruit, specifically strawberries and various melons, for breakfast. I personally didn't care for them, but the moment I saw her face almost dry heave by looking at the plate of fruit, I knew something was wrong. She narrowed it down to a bad batch.

I smiled and knew our careless night after my trip to Boston resulted in another Edwards baby.

Charlotte made the pregnancy look easy, though I would never discredit just how difficult it was. We were both juggling an inquisitive toddler who had no sense of fear. We never expected Amelia to be such a little dare-devil. It wasn't uncommon to find her attempting to climb over her crib or reaching on the countertop for something she shouldn't be eating. I knew it drove Charlotte absolutely insane. When it comes to parenting styles, Charlotte is more disciplinary than me. Perhaps, you could say I have a soft spot for my daughter. When your child is surrounded by so much family, it's only natural she would be spoiled.

I break free of my thoughts, clutching onto Charlotte's hand as the doctors examine her.

She was brought in only an hour ago after being found in a ditch where she gave birth to our daughter.

My mind refuses to push aside the image of *him* beside her. So many questions were left unanswered, which only fueled the rage inside me. My heart is beating so fast, unable to slow down from the adrenaline pumping through my blood.

I'm supposed to focus on my wife and child.

But I want him *dead*.

My gut instincts warned me something was off for the last few months. It's why I confronted him inside his office even though he flat-out lied to my face and made me look like I was insane.

Charlotte argued I was losing the plot. It started too many fights, so I learned to keep my mouth shut, not wanting another wedge between us. It didn't mean I'd forgotten. I made sure he wasn't anywhere near her.

But obviously, I fucked up somehow.

The baby is wheeled into the NICU so the doctors can examine her too. Charlotte's eyes widen in panic, begging she go with her.

"Charlotte," I whisper, caressing her cheek. "She's going to be fine. It's just precautionary."

Deep breaths escape Charlotte's dry lips as she nods while trying to calm herself down. The doctors continue to poke and prod, but my mind refuses to focus.

Suddenly, my parents rush through the doors. Mom reaches out her hand, quick to touch my arm as Dad goes into doctor mode.

"Honey," Mom says softly. "Where's the baby?"

"NICU," I choke, unable to hide my anguish. "She's going to be okay."

Mom breathes a sigh of relief. "Of course, she's going to be okay. Someone is watching over our family."

Now is probably not the time to give Mom the complete rundown on how this occurred. The skin around my eyes bunch as I stare at Charlotte. Aside from some cuts and bruises, all her limbs are intact, given the severity of the accident and the damage to the car.

I should have been there. Why did I let this happen?

"Lex, you look tired," Mom mentions with a concerned voice. "Why don't you go outside and grab a coffee? I'll be right here with Charlie."

"I... I can't leave now."

Charlotte clears her throat. "Please get some coffee. It's

going to be a long night, and your mom is right here. I'm clearly not going anywhere."

"I'll check on the baby."

"Sounds like a good plan." Charlotte smiles weakly.

"Mom, please call me if you need me. I'll be ten minutes."

Mom nods as I kiss Charlotte on the forehead before stepping out into the corridor. The moment the door shuts behind me, the adrenalin rushes through me again. There's a pounding in my ears, followed by the sound of sirens. My eyes shut tight, unable to rid myself of the memory of seeing Charlotte lying on the dirt.

"There he is," a familiar voice says.

I lift my gaze to see Eric and Rocky walking toward me. I'm not surprised Eric is here but wonder why Rocky is, given he mentioned nothing about visiting the West Coast.

"Dude, what the hell happened?" Rocky questions with his arms crossed.

Struggling to swallow the giant lump inside my throat, a slight guttural roar escapes instead.

"*Him...*" I grit.

Eric curls his hand into a fist, pressing it against his mouth. "Lex, calm down. The important thing is everyone is alive."

"*I will not calm down,*" I shout, my voice echoing in the long corridor. "How long has he been stalking her? Was his intent to kidnap her and ..."

"Don't say it, man." Rocky shakes his head. "Baker never came across like that. He's just not over Charlie. He wouldn't harm her."

I push Rocky's chest, releasing my anger. "How the fuck do you know that?"

"You guys." Eric panics, trying to pull my arm, but he's

doing a pathetic job at it. "I'm not equipped to handle heterosexual fights. If you pulled his hair or something, I'd be breaking this up in a heartbeat."

Rocky raises his hands in the air, calling defeat. Instead, I lean against the wall, shutting my eyes to control my rage.

"I know you don't want to face the facts, but he saved her life and your baby," Rocky tells me bluntly. "You can wish he was dead, but chances are, so would your family."

My eyes dart to his, painfully trying to come to terms with the truth. Chances are, this was out of my control. Charlotte's contraction caused the accident. If he wasn't following her, she'd be *dead*.

The door opens as Dad exits the room. "There you are. Have you had a chance to visit the baby?"

I scratch my head, letting out a heavy sigh. "I'm about to head over."

Dad places his hand on my shoulder, glancing over at Rocky and Eric, who watch on cautiously, half-expecting me to lash out again. Instead, my shoulders fall, the exhaustion from the mental anguish suddenly overcoming me.

"I'll go check on the baby. Then, provided there's nothing concerning, I'll bring her over," he suggests, keeping his expression fixed. "Go be with Charlie. Your mother is trying to convince her to book a holiday, but we all know it's because she wants to steal her grandkids."

His hand leaves my shoulder then he walks toward the NICU.

"Look, I'm going to forgive you for trying to knock me out," Rocky says calmly. "But we all know I can kick your ass, Edwards."

"A cock fight would have been perfect." Eric grins.

Rocky furrows his brows. "You're a sick mother fucker. You know that?"

"I'm not the one who enjoys perusing photos of women's feet. If anyone is sick and twisted, it's you, Rockford Romano."

I stare at them both, wondering what the fuck is wrong with them. At the same time, Rocky scans the corridor, then retrieves a flask from his jacket.

"Here, drink some. It'll take the edge off."

He unscrews the cap, and instantly, the scent of smokey whisky lingers.

"I'm supposed to be getting coffee."

Rocky snorts. "Coffee? You pussy. Drink it. You'll feel much better."

Despite my better judgment, I take it from his hands and take a long-winded swig. The burn sliding down my throat is exactly what I need to calm myself down. As soon as I'm done, I let out a loud rasp.

"So, are we all okay?" Eric questions with a prolonged stare.

Both Rocky and I nod in unison. Then Eric claps his hands in delight.

"Should we all kiss and make up?"

"You're fucked up," Rocky berates him. "You better not jerk off to photos of me."

Eric rolls his eyes in disgust. "Please, I have taste when it comes to my jerking-off fantasies."

I don't want to partake in this conversation anymore. If I've learned anything over the last two years, it's that these two have no filters or boundaries during conversations.

Taking a deep breath, I'm much calmer as the whisky settles in. I push the door open and see Charlotte lying on the bed with a hopeful gaze. She's eager to hold the baby, so I'm praying Dad won't be too much longer.

The door opens to Dad pushing a plastic crib into the room. Mom lets out a sigh as does Charlotte.

"I've got someone special wanting to meet everyone." Dad smiles proudly.

Mom hovers around the crib, then lifts the baby in her arms to pass to Charlotte.

"She's just beautiful. Do we have a name?"

"Ava," I say softly, glancing at Charlotte, knowing how much she loves the name.

Charlotte's lips curve into a relaxed smile. "So, we're going with the tradition of names starting with A? I thought you hated that?'

"Hmm," I murmur, looking at Ava. "Maybe I might feel different when we have the next kid."

"Next kid?" Charlotte blurts out.

"How about we give you two a moment with your daughter," Dad suggests, then quickly ushers Mom outside.

Alone with Charlotte and Ava, I choose my words carefully.

"I know we don't have to decide now, but maybe another baby wouldn't be so bad."

"How about we talk about this when my vagina isn't torn up?" Charlotte notes with dark amusement. "Push me, and you're getting the snip."

I rest my hand on her arm. "Hormones look beautiful on you."

Charlotte breaks out into a smile. "You're lucky you're so damn good-looking."

"I guess it helps," I tease.

The second the words leave my mouth, Charlotte moves her face closer, wrinkling her nose.

"Have you been drinking?"

"Not drinking. I had a small serving."

"Where?" she demands, then rolls her eyes. "Rocky is here?"

"How did you know?"

"Nikki just sent me a text. Apparently, he was in Vegas for some boxing match then took a private plane as soon as he heard."

"Eric's outside too," I inform her.

All of a sudden, her face turns panicked. "Amelia?"

"Mom left her with Adriana. She texted me when she was on her way here with Dad."

Charlotte's shoulders relax. At the same time, Ava makes a little sound.

"She's perfect, looks just like you." Charlotte sighs dreamily. "I bet she has your eyes."

"She has your nose."

"Your stubbornness."

I cock my head with a grin. "Your stubbornness, Mrs. Edwards."

We both fall silent, admiring our newest addition. Then, Charlotte turns to face me.

"Lex, we need to talk about what happened."

This moment needs to be perfect, and if it means we don't discuss what happened, then I'm going to make sure *he* has no power over me. The fucker has interfered too many times, and I refuse for him to take this moment away from me.

"Shh," I whisper, caressing Ava's soft hair. "Let's enjoy our little miracle."

"Are you going to still call her that when she's sixteen and begging you to allow her to have a boyfriend?"

I glimpse down at her peaceful tiny face as she sleeps.

"Ava is going to be my little angel," I tell Charlotte. "Daddy's well-behaved and respectful girl."

"You bet your life on it?" Charlotte muses.

A grin spreads across my face. "Sure, why not? I'm always right."

"Something tells me you're in for a rude awakening," Charlotte warns playfully. "An all-girl Dad. You're in big trouble, Mr. Edwards. Really big trouble..."

FOURTEEN

The time when I 'apparently' couldn't keep my dick in my pants

"No, no, no..."

Charlotte paces the bathroom shaking her head. "This is all your fault."

I knew Charlotte falling pregnant would somehow be my fault, even though she never complained during the multiple orgasms when I was fucking her that night when the kids stayed with my parents.

"No one's to blame."

Her nostrils flare as she points her finger at me. "You're to blame. You're the one with a degree in medicine."

"What does that have to do with it?" I argue, knowing very well I'm playing with fire right now.

She places her hands on her hips, annoyed with me. Only now, I notice the red stain on her shirt from when Amelia spilled cranberry juice. Ava slipped into the mess, which resulted in her being covered in the sticky liquid. Then, of course, she needed cuddles.

"You should have known the antibiotics I was taking for the flu would somehow affect my pill."

"Everyone knows that."

Charlotte's eyes widen in disbelief. "Everyone knows that?"

"You know what I mean."

"No, explain how everyone knows that, and by everyone, you mean you?" She rushes in a frustrated tone. "You still fucked me!"

"Will you calm down? So, we're having another kid. You're a great mother."

Charlotte bows her head while shaking it, then lets out a huff. "I woke up at four this morning just to get work in. I tried to shower but the girls' wanted pancakes. In case you haven't noticed, we had a juice incident. I'm not sure what's in my hair, but I suspect it's candy from when I fell asleep on the couch and didn't realize Amelia left it there."

She has a point. Our life is chaos with these two girls. Whoever said girls are easy is a fucking liar. Sometimes, when I need a moment, I visit Adriana and spend time with Andy because he's such a relaxed kid.

Apparently, we procreated a spawn from the devil. Ava, I can't fault. She's innocent until her big sister gets involved.

"We'll get through this. We always do," I assure her.

"Yeah, we'll get through this." Charlotte air quotes. "There's no 'we' when you're at your office and traveling the world."

I bite my tongue to refrain from debating this fact, but I'm a stubborn man and open my mouth. "Traveling the world is extreme. When was the last time I left the country?"

"Uh, how about two months ago when you went to Hong Kong and Amelia caught chicken pox?"

"I flew back as soon as you told me," I remind her.

Charlotte throws her hands in the air. "What about me, Lex? Have you ever stopped to think about my career?"

My hand reaches out to Charlotte's waist as I try to pull her toward me, but she won't budge. Instantly, I remove my hands from her since it's clear she wants nothing to do with me right now.

"We can hire help."

With a sneer, Charlotte juts her chin and crosses her arms. "Money doesn't fix everything."

There's a loud bang on the bathroom door, followed by Amelia storming in.

"We're going to be late for Andy's birthday party," Amelia pouts, placing her hands on her hips.

Ava runs in, stumbling on her feet as I race over to pick her up from the ground before she cries.

"I need a minute," Charlotte answers with resignation.

"Sixty seconds?" Amelia questions then raises her voice, "One, two, three—"

I glance at Charlotte, noticing she's on the verge of a breakdown. With Ava in my arms, I usher Amelia out of the bathroom.

"How about we let Mommy get ready in peace? If we're a few minutes late, Andy won't mind."

"But, Daddy!" Amelia complains in a high-pitched tone. "I want to play in the bouncy castle!"

This kid will be the death of me. I take a deep breath, trying to remain calm. Charlotte's right. Three kids are a lot. *What the hell was I thinking blowing inside her?*

"Good things come to those who wait," I tell her. "Now, sit quietly in the kitchen and wait until Mommy is ready. If you interrupt her again, we're both in trouble. You understand?"

Amelia rolls her eyes in annoyance. "Yes, Daddy."

Addison was born at the stroke of midday after a quick labor. According to Charlotte, Addison's birth was the least painful of all the girls.

Thankfully, it was only an overnight stay in the hospital, so we encouraged everyone to hold their visits until we arrived home.

On the drive home, I thought it was best to warn Charlotte of the surprise party Adriana and Eric have thrown for her and the baby.

"Listen, as your husband, I need to let you know Adriana and Eric have planned a surprise party for you."

Charlotte glances at me with a tired face, though I'm forced to look away and focus on the road.

"I look like shit."

"You look beautiful."

A yawn escapes her. "You have to say that. You want pussy."

"Pussy is out of the question for six weeks," I remind her with a chuckle. "However, if you said ass..."

Charlotte laughs, then winces. "My vagina hurts when I laugh. Why the party?"

"Because you didn't want a baby shower. I told you this would happen."

"I didn't see the point," she admits while staring out the window. "We have everything from Amelia and Ava. The bonus of having all girls."

"Speaking of all girls..."

She shakes her head almost immediately. "If this is

about trying for a boy, I swear to God I will cut your dick off right now."

A fake smile spreads across my face. "Pleasant. No, it's about school. Have you thought more about Amelia attending an all-girls school?"

"Look, you don't understand how a young girl's mind works. Take boys out of the equation, and all they can think about is boys."

"That makes no sense," I chastise.

"Yes, because you're a man. Your brain works differently. So, to answer your question, I think Amelia will thrive in a co-ed school."

We drive onto our property as I pull up next to the front door. It's a warm summer's day, typical Californian weather. The sun is shining brightly, burning my skin as I step out of our SUV. I quickly move around to the passenger side to assist Charlotte. When she's safely out, I unbuckle the carrier and gently remove Addison from the car.

"How are we able to produce such perfect-looking little girls?" I ask, beguiled by the tiny little face sleeping so peacefully. "I think she'll definitely have your eyes."

Charlotte snorts. "My boring brown ones against your emerald? Fat chance."

Before we enter, I hold Charlotte back. "Remember to act surprised."

"Yes, sir."

My spare hand reaches out for the door as everyone yells surprise! Charlotte slaps her hands on her cheeks, forcing a shocked face.

"What in the world," she exclaims.

Eric draws his brows, then crosses his arms with pouting lips. "You knew! That was the worst fake face ever."

"Well, I just pushed a baby out of my vagina. What do you want from me?" Charlotte complains.

Everyone moves closer to gather around us, trying to catch a glimpse of Addison.

"She's beautiful," Mom says, wiping a proud lonesome tear from her face.

Dad places his hand on my shoulder. "Good work, son."

Adriana is quick to pull a face. "Good work, son? Lex did nothing. The last I heard he didn't suddenly grow a uterus."

"Technically..." Eric begins with, "Mr. Winkle needed to drop his tinkle to make a baby, so..."

"Who is Mr. Winkle?" Amelia asks loudly.

I shoot an annoyed stare at Eric.

"Sweetheart, would you like to meet your sister?" I ask to distract Amelia.

My knees crouch so I'm at Amelia and Ava's height. Amelia looks less than pleased that another child will fight her for attention.

"She's fine, so about Mr. Winkle?" Amelia drags, uninterested in the baby.

Charlotte moves closer to Amelia. "You know, being the biggest sister can be a lot of fun too."

"How?"

"Well, for starters, you're going to be the first to do a lot of things."

"Like have a boyfriend?" Amelia questions then turns to Eric.

"Look, I don't know why she just looked at me." Eric raises his hands, playing innocent. He's notorious for being a bad influence and trying to teach her new things, which in my opinion are not age appropriate.

"Sure, one day, if Daddy doesn't unalive them first," Charlotte mutters.

Ava reaches out her hand, gently caressing Addison's face. "My baby."

We always knew Amelia would have reservations once the baby came home. Of late, she's been playing up to garner our attention. Most of the time, she'll blame Ava, but we know who is behind it.

"How about I go spend some time with Amelia?" Charlotte mentions quietly.

"Good idea."

Poor Addison is passed around to each of our family members. It gives me an opportunity to take a small break, knowing tonight may be a sleepless night with all three girls settling into the new routine.

Mom and Adriana have outdone themselves with the food. I hadn't realized how famished I was until I walked into the dining room and saw platters of food, all of which looked incredibly delicious.

We take turns eating. Then, I make sure the girls eat to distract them while Charlotte feeds Addison. When night falls, everyone says goodbye, and I'm glad for the peace and quiet.

Amelia and Ava are tired after running around with Andy. Ava falls asleep as soon as she's bathed, and her head hits the pillow. Amelia, though, she's wide awake.

"Daddy, I don't want any more babies in the house."

I force a smile, not sure how to tackle this conversation.

"It's nice to have a big family, lots of love to go around," I inform her.

Amelia crosses her arms. "I can give more love so we don't have any more babies."

"That's not quite how it works."

"Why?"

"Because God's plan may be different."

'But why?" she questions again.

"Amelia, sweetheart, it's late. How about we read a story and then go to sleep? There's plenty more time tomorrow for questions."

"I'm not tired."

"Okay." I nod, then grab a book from her shelf. "I'll just read for fun."

Not even a quarter into the book, Amelia's eyes begin to droop. I glance over, smiling at her sleeping face. I don't blame her for feeling this way, but I didn't expect her to be so resistant to a new baby.

When she's fast asleep, I tuck Amelia into her special blanket, then turn the light off. I quickly check on Ava, who is still fast asleep. With quiet steps, I walk toward our bedroom to find Charlotte in bed breastfeeding Addison.

"How did you go?"

I rub my chin, then let out a yawn. "Which answer will make you happy?"

Charlotte releases a sigh. "She's still upset, isn't she?"

"Amelia is stubborn."

"Yeah, but we can't ignore how she feels," Charlotte points out.

My fingers begin to unbutton my shirt before I remove it to go shower. Charlotte's eyes wander down my torso, but she quickly turns away.

"I'm not saying ignore Amelia. We just need to take turns in making sure we spend time with her so she doesn't feel the baby has taken over."

"Right, we should do that."

I make my way toward the bathroom for a shower. Under the hot water, my muscles relax so much that it's a struggle to get out. After drying myself off, placing my on boxers, then brushing my teeth, I head back into the room for bed.

Addison is in her bassinet beside the bed, fast asleep from the milk coma she's found herself in. Last night, she slept for four hours straight, but I know the second night is always the worst.

"Do you need anything?" I ask before climbing into bed.

Charlotte's intense stare catches my attention.

"You."

A half-laugh escapes me. "Funny, you're off-limits."

I climb into bed, getting myself comfortable. Then, Charlotte places her hand on my thigh, sliding it up between my legs.

"You're not off-limits," she teases.

My head tilts with curiosity. "That's true, but don't you think you should be resting since you just had a baby?"

"It's the hormones," she blurts out. "It's confusing."

I scratch my jaw with a smirk playing on my lips. "So, you're horny but obviously out for the next six weeks. If I understand this correctly, you want to blow me because that's all you can do right now?"

Charlotte rests her hand on my cock, which instantly goes hard.

"Yeah, you got a problem with that, Mr. Edwards?"

My hands reach for the top of my boxers, yanking them down to free my cock.

"Not a single problem at all..."

FIFTEEN

The time when the universe had other plans

"Will you stop worrying about it? This is not for you to get involved."

Charlotte stares blankly at the suitcases on the bed. She's usually organized and packed well before any trip, taking charge of everyone's items with some fancy app she uses to make sure everything is ticked off and nothing is left behind.

"They're family," she reminds me with a heavy sigh. "I don't understand how it doesn't bother you at all that we're flying all the way to Sydney, Australia, just to celebrate Rocky's birthday, and we're leaving Nikki behind."

I pinch the bridge of my nose. This is all we've been discussing for months. No matter what I say, the answer won't satisfy her or fix the problem.

Mainly because it's not *our* problem to fix.

"We're not leaving her behind. Nikki chose not to come given their circumstances."

Much to my annoyance, Charlotte plonks herself on the bed and stops packing. It's obvious we're going to continue talking about this. Mindful of the time, I give Charlotte my attention but keep note of how long until we need to leave.

"I don't understand how this happened."

I sit beside her, resting my arms on my legs, then begin to rub my face. My mouth opens to speak, but then it closes. Rocky and Nikki's separation wasn't a surprise to me, they'd been butting heads for a long time. The last year was strained, given Rocky accepted a new job at a big network and Nikki was taking on more clients since the firm grew so much on the East Coast.

Nikki is known to keep her emotions to herself, always putting on a brave front, especially in front of Charlotte. Unlike Rocky, too many drunken rants, and when he's on a roll, he will tell you every last detail, from what they argued over to who showered the longest.

Given they lived on the East Coast, it wasn't like we saw them all the time. The distance was often welcoming when it came to those two. It's difficult being in the same space as two people who have no issue arguing in front of you.

"They had a kid young. Who you are in college is not always who you are later on in life," I try to explain without starting our own argument.

"I know," Charlotte resigns, looking at me oddly.

"Why are you looking at me that way?"

"The Alex I fell in love with, who had graduated college, is far different from the man I married."

Silence falls over me. I would never want to return to being a coward who couldn't stand up for himself nor fight for who he loved. The old me allowed others to dictate my life and future when it should have been me all along who made such important decisions.

"Look, Charlotte. You need to step away and not put yourself in the middle of them. They're adults, and they've made a big decision to separate."

Charlotte throws her hands in the air in frustration. "But don't you see? They both wanted the same thing... another child. And look what's happened? It's torn them apart."

"You said it yourself. Infertility can often drive couples apart."

She wrings her hands, trying to come to terms with reality. "It never ceases to amaze me how every couple's journey is different. They tried to fall pregnant for years, and nothing, even after trying IVF multiple times. You only have to look at me, and I fall pregnant."

A small smile settles on my lips. Then I grab her hand to kiss it. "I love you, but please stop stressing yourself out. Nikki is bringing Will and staying with our girls. Everything will work out."

The truth is, I have no idea if it will all work out, but for now, I need Charlotte to focus on us. With a long-winded sigh, she continues to pack our suitcases while I make sure all our electronics and charges are packed securely. When she's done, I take the suitcases downstairs.

"Bitches," Rocky roars while walking inside the kitchen. Amelia and Ava's eyes widen as he realizes they're standing right there. "Damn. Sorry, girls."

"You know, Uncle Rocky. You shouldn't refer to a woman in such derogatory terms."

Rocky scratches his head. "How old are you again?"

"Old enough to tell you you're being chauvinistic—"

"Amelia, enough," I gently scold her.

"But, Daddy, he's being rude," Amelia argues with her hands on her hips.

"Yeah, Daddy," Ava agrees with her.

"Well, technically, I wasn't referring to any woman. I was referring to Daddy." Rocky snickers.

"Why would you call Daddy a bitch?" Ava asks.

The door opens again, but this time it's Eric. I don't think I've been this happy to see him, hoping his arrival distracts the girls.

"Hello, mates," Eric greets with an awful Aussie accent. "Are you ready to have a shrimp on the barbie?"

"Uncle Rocky?" Ava pauses to examine Eric. "Is Uncle Eric a bitch?"

This time, I try to hold back my smile.

"Kid, you have no idea how much." Rocky chuckles.

Charlotte walks in, dressed in a pair of jeans and a sweater since the plane ride is fourteen hours long. I opted to wear jeans and a sweater, too, since it's just our group on the private plane I hired. I'm lucky Charlotte didn't argue, given I've wanted to buy a private plane for years. Of course, she insisted the money could be put to better use and gave me a long list of organizations needing financial aid.

So, the compromise is to hire one for long-haul flights.

"You guys are here," she greets, then raises her brows. "Wait, where's Tristan?"

Eric purses his lips. "About him, a last-minute job in Palm Springs. He can't come."

"Okay." Charlotte nods with slight disappointment. "So, Adriana and Julian will meet us at the airport. All we're waiting for is Kate to come to pick up the girls."

"I can't believe Noah and Kate offered to take care of the girls," Eric muses.

"It's only four days, then Nikki stays with them for the other four." As soon as it leaves Charlotte's mouth, she glances quietly at Rocky. "Will is coming too to help Nikki."

"Will is coming?" Amelia asks, her eyes lighting up while she rubs her hands like she has some evil plan for him.

Charlotte presses her lips together. "Amelia, I want you on your best behavior. Will is a good boy, and I don't want to hear that you're getting him into trouble."

"I hate to break it to you, kid..." Rocky says with amusement, "...Will probably won't pay much attention to you since he's too busy breaking girls' hearts."

Ava gasps. "Break a girl's heart! How?"

Eric bends down. "Sweetie pie, one day, Uncle Eric is going to explain to you all the terrible things boys and girls do to each other. We'll start with Daddy and Mommy's story and a little story I'd like to call a complicated love triangle..."

Kate enters through the back door, her timing perfect as usual. She lets out an unwarranted laugh when she notices my relieved expression.

"Aunty Kate!" the girls yell excitedly in unison.

"Are you guys ready for the best four days of your life?"

Charlotte touches Kate's arm. "Are you sure you're going to be okay? You have Sienna to care for, plus Jessa and Nash."

"Nash is with Olivia for the week," Kate informs her. "Jessa wanted to be with her cousins. Trust me. We'll be fine."

We say goodbye to the girls, hugging them each and reminding them to be on their best behavior. Amelia and Ava have zero care in the world, eager for their sleepover. Addison pulls on my sleeve with sad eyes.

"Daddy, I love you."

"I love you too, baby girl."

Charlotte's eyes haze over, making it my cue to get us out of here before she chickens out.

"It's only eight days," I remind her.

"Eight days of Aussie birds." Rocky cheers.

"Birds?" Eric cringes. "That's so crass, and I think that's British, not Aussie."

"Are we ready, bitches?" Rocky questions with a grin.

"If it'll get you out of here..." I tell him, "... then yes, let's go."

Rocky almost drinks half a bottle of bourbon despite me telling him to slow down. We're only five hours into our fourteen-hour flight, and everyone is asleep except the birthday boy, Julian, who is reading a book, and me.

Rocky grows eerily quiet. "She's seeing someone."

I lift my head, unsure how to respond. Julian also raises his eyes from his book, glancing at me momentarily.

"Yesterday, she asked to see me." Rocky grips the glass tightly. "He's a banker. Can you believe that? It's like she purposely wanted to hurt me."

Watching the woman you love with another man is the greatest pain of all. Hell, I should know.

"You both agreed to separate," I remind him gently.

Rocky keeps his eyes fixated on the glass. "I know."

"Are you having second thoughts just because she's seeing someone?"

"She's my wife," he mutters beneath this breath. "She just moved on like we were nothing."

"In all fairness, it's been six months," I note, eyeing him dubiously, praying he doesn't lash out and throw his drink at the wall in anger. "You can't tell us you've been celibate."

Rocky's eyes dart to mine. "I haven't touched a single woman since we separated."

I'm surprised by his admission. Although I never asked directly, I assumed the first thing he would have done was fuck some other woman. Two or three at a time, knowing him.

Julian clears his throat. "If you think there's a chance for the two of you, then you need to be honest. Or else this banker, as you refer to him, will take what is yours."

The irony of this conversation is not lost on me. While the years have been easier to tolerate Julian given he is Adriana's husband, I never forgot the past. Some memories will stick forever, especially if those memories are part of your darkest days.

"I'm going to agree. This isn't the time to hold back your feelings. You have a family. If you're going to fight, this is the time."

"Yeah, or I just give her what she wants... a divorce."

Rocky drinks the remnants of the glass before closing his eyes and passing out.

Adriana made sure our time in Sydney was spent wisely.

We did all the tourist attractions like seeing the Habour Bridge and Opera House. Somehow, she convinced us to visit Taronga Zoo. I don't care for zoos, but watching Eric get shit on by a koala has so far been the highlight of the trip. The fact that it happened on his expensive loafers is even better.

The weather has been perfect. Blue skies and warm

weather but not overly hot. It's not my first visit to Sydney, having been here a few times. It never ceases to amaze me how friendly the people are, always willing to offer directions or just general help.

"That Aussie chick was trying to pick you up," Charlotte points out as we walk along the quay. "Did you tip her?"

Rocky knocks into me with a cocky grin. "He sure tipped her."

"What's that supposed to mean?" Charlotte asks, narrowing her eyes at him.

"It means I thanked her monetarily for her good service," I assure her. Though it's sexy, she's jealous.

"The tip was big," Rocky continues to provoke Charlotte. "Mr. Billionaire made sure she was taken care of."

"Gross, Rocky," Adriana complains. "How is it possible that you can make anything sound dirty?"

"It's one of my many talents," he responds proudly. "Test me. Give me something to say that is not dirty, and I'll make sure you're creaming your pants when I'm done."

Adriana screws up her face, then her face lights up. "Eric's Gucci loafers smell like koala dung."

Rocky clears his throat, followed by pouting his lips. *"Eric's Gucci loafers smell like Koala dung."*

Charlotte bursts out laughing. "The look on Eric's face when the koala pooped."

Eric crosses his arms with annoyance. "It wasn't even proper shit. It was some sort of weird koala diarrhea. They could have told me he wasn't feeling great."

"Hey, hey, hey," Rocky raises his voice, demanding attention. "So, how did I rate?"

"Surprisingly well," Adriana quips. "Though not enough to make me cream my pants."

"Guess I'll leave that for my date tonight."

Everyone slows their steps, the girls coming to a complete stop. Oddly so, Eric focuses on the ground. I prepare myself for the interrogation. Charlotte and Adriana are relentless when they want to be.

"Date?" Charlotte repeats in a heated tone. "I don't understand."

"What's there to understand?" Rocky shrugs, keeping his gaze fixed on the people walking past. "I met someone, and we're going on a date."

"You've met someone? We've been here for three days, all of which you've been with us," Charlotte informs him. Then, she turns to face me. "Did you know about this?"

I raise my hands in defeat. "No, I've been with you."

"When did this happen?" Adriana butts in.

"If you must know, last night. After you guys left, Eric and I stayed for more drinks."

The girls turn to look at Eric. Adriana is the first to open her mouth.

"You knew about this and never said anything?"

Eric lets out an annoyed huff. "There was never time."

"You spoke to me and Adriana for the entire drive to Bondi Beach about your fear of bunions." Charlotte dead-pans, shaking her head. "Then you started discussing various foot fungal infections, including the one you once claimed you caught from this French guy who loved to swim in public pools."

"Don't blame him, okay?" Rocky says, keeping his expression blank. "I know what you guys are thinking, and I'm hoping you had the same reaction when Nikki told you she's fucking some new banker guy."

Adriana clears her throat. "She's not fucking him, just seeing him."

"Have you seen my wife?" Rocky argues back. "Sorry, ex-wife. She's hot."

This conversation is getting worse by the minute. Charlotte was right. Maybe this trip wasn't the best idea.

"We have dinner reservations in less than ten minutes," I inform everyone wishing to change subjects. "If you must talk, at least try to walk faster, please."

Charlotte and Adriana remain quiet for the rest of the walk. By the time we reach the restaurant, we're only a few minutes late.

It comes as no surprise the girls smash the wine. I have a glass myself, but judging by Charlotte's intake, I'm going to have one drunk wife tonight. Just fucking great.

When it's time for Rocky to leave, Charlotte is the first to say something.

"Have fun on your date. Make sure you use a condom," she announces, too loudly that people glance at us.

"Yeah, you know what you catch from a stranger's pussy?" Adriana laughs, almost falling off her chair. "Crabs, for one."

Eric cringes as he pushes the plate of food, which happens to be crab, into the middle of the table. "And there goes my appetite."

Rocky doesn't entertain them. He simply grins, then nods goodbye.

I glance over at Julian, who, just like me, now must deal with an intoxicated wife.

"I think we should head back to the hotel," I suggest, then raise my hand to motion for the waiter to return with our bill.

The walk back to the hotel isn't far, but the girls struggle to walk in a straight line, singing some Abba song I don't care for. Charlotte resists going back to the room, wanting to drink with Adriana in the lobby. Given there's a group of Aussie soccer players all drinking at the bar, it's a hard no from me.

Back in the room, Charlotte lets out a huff as soon as the door closes.

"Well, you're a party pooper."

"Your karma will pay a visit tomorrow morning," I remind her.

Just as she's about to argue with me, her phone begins to ring. She glances at the caller ID, then bites her lips. "Uh, oh."

"Who is it?"

She raises the phone, so I can read. Nikki's name flashes on the screen.

"Answer it. It might be important since she's with the girls."

"But what about Rocky?"

"For the love of God, Charlotte. Answer the fucking phone."

Charlotte lets out a deep breath, pressing answer and putting Nikki on speaker.

"Hey," she greets cautiously.

"Charlie, we need to talk," Nikki rushes in a panicked voice.

Charlotte sits on the edge of the bed. "Is everything okay with the girls?"

"The girls are fine. Will is taking care of them downstairs. I'm in your bathroom."

We both glance at each other, unsure why she's panicked inside our bathroom.

"My bathroom?" Charlotte questions as her face pales. "Is everything okay?"

"I'm pregnant," Nikki blurts out.

My eyes widen in shock, unable to process the news. At the same time, Charlotte stares at me with a distressed expression before she throws her head forward and vomits all over the floor.

Just fucking great.

SIXTEEN

The time when we decided no more children

All three girls finally fell asleep after all the excitement of us arriving back home.

We walk into our bedroom, barely able to move a limb from the long flight to then coming home and spending time with the girls. We'd brought home some gifts, including Australian chocolate, which was devoured too quickly. It explains why they've been bouncing off the walls all day.

Our day has been nonstop since we landed at six this morning, and even though I'm a seasoned traveler, I'm utterly exhausted right now.

A yawn escapes Charlotte as we climb into bed which then onsets one on my behalf.

"How do our kids have so much energy? Do you even remember being a kid and running around all day long?"

No," I respond with a smile. "But I do remember having a little sister who gave the Energizer bunny a run for his money."

Charlotte laughs softly. "Adriana had a lot of energy. She still does, actually. Speaking of which…"

I fix my pillow to get more comfortable. "Hmm…"

"This whole Nikki being pregnant thing—"

"Is not for you to get involved," I interrupt, reminding her again.

"No, I meant, I don't think I want any more kids."

This isn't the first time we've had this discussion, but as the girls got older and more demanding, the conversation became more frequent. It came up when Kate fell pregnant and again when one of Charlotte's colleagues found out she was pregnant only a few weeks ago.

"You don't think, or you know?" I question her sternly. "Big difference, Charlotte."

She bows her head, then releases a weighted sigh.

"I don't know," Charlotte mumbles while toying with her wedding ring. "I mean, do you want more kids?"

We have a great life, and even with three girls, we're managing to just balance it all. There have been so many sacrifices on both our parts, but if I'm honest, I miss my wife and spending time with her. With three kids, it's getting harder to find time for us.

"I'm happy with our family right now, but I'm not sure I'm able to make permanent decisions. We're still young."

Charlotte simply nods, listening attentively. "A vasectomy is reversal if we change our minds later."

Far be it for me to be a pussy, but the thought of having my balls operated on is less than appealing. Perhaps I should practice the art of pulling out. *Who are you fucking kidding right now?*

"I know you're thinking you can just pull out," she admonishes, then pats my hand with a mocking smile. "Baby, your pull-out game is your weakness. I mean, who would have thought the great Lex Edwards has a weakness?"

"Very funny." My hand jabs the side of her rib, and she jumps from being ticklish. "Do we have to talk about this now? I'm tired."

"Yes, because we have an appointment tomorrow afternoon."

My head turns abruptly as my eyes widen in shock. *She said what now?* Suddenly, between my legs feels incredibly uncomfortable, like someone kicked me in the nuts.

"You booked an appointment for me to get the snip tomorrow?"

"No, I booked an appointment to consult with a specialist about getting the snip. You know how it all works."

I cross my arms in defiance. "I know how it fucking works. I studied medicine."

"I know you did..." she reaffirms before glancing my way again. "Look, it's just a consult."

There are many things in our marriage that I give in to. Charlotte not wanting nannies or full-time hired help. We compromised earlier in our marriage and have a cleaner once a week, plus a gardener who also takes care of the pool. The couple are married, and Charlotte met them through her work with a foundation. If I could have had my way, they would be employed full-time as well as a nanny to help with the girls.

But no, Charlotte insisted we raise these girls ourselves. If we needed a babysitter, we asked our family or friends. Most of the time, we swap with Adriana since she also runs her own business and has flexible schedules.

"You've ambushed me with this consult, and for all I

know, they'll wheel me into a room and cut into my balls without my permission," I argue.

Charlotte huffs. "Now you're being dramatic. Fine, have it your way. Don't go. I'll stay on the pill and screw my body up so you can have glorious orgasms and not have to pull out. How does that sound?"

There's no reasoning with her because we're too far into this argument. With a sudden headache striking me, I turn around with my back facing her, then turn off the lamp.

They say you shouldn't go to bed angry.

But they weren't married to Charlotte Edwards.

"Are you ready, Mr. Edwards?"

There have only been a few times in my life when nerves overcame me. This is one of those moments. A god damn knife is going to cut into my balls. Aside from the fear of pain, what if they damage something and I'm unable to come like a normal man? *What if my dick is ruined, and I can't get hard?*

I'm dressed in a pair of sweats and tee, ready to head into the room to change into a gown. Charlotte is standing beside me, staring oddly with a pale face. All morning, she's been looking unwell, but I narrowed it down to nerves on her end.

"Are you okay?" I ask, observing her face closer. Her eyes appear dull, and even her lips look pale.

She nods with pursed lips. "I'm fine ... it's just ..."

I wait for her response, but she quickly presses her hand over her mouth and rushes to the trash can in the corner of the room. The violent sounds of her vomiting profusely worry me. I run over, rubbing her back, allowing her to empty her stomach.

The door opens as a nurse checks in on us.

"Can you please give us a minute?" I demand, pulling Charlotte's hair away from her face. "My wife is unwell."

"Of course, would you like some water, Mrs. Edwards?"

Charlotte shakes her head, keeping her words at bay.

"How about you bring some anyway?"

The nurse closes the door as Charlotte lifts her head while attempting to take deep breaths.

"You've looked pale all morning. Maybe it's not nerves. It could be a stomach bug. The daycare always has something new spreading."

Charlotte closes her eyes, then winces. Her hands move to her stomach as she clutches it, obviously in pain.

"Okay, look at me," I beg of her, now worried. "Show me where it hurts?"

She drops her hand toward her stomach, and then she inches lower.

"Why don't we have a doctor check you out? We are in a hospital," I remind her.

"But you're a doctor," Charlotte croaks. "You check me out."

I grab onto her arm, concerned she may faint. "Baby, I'm not equipped, and I'm worried. This vasectomy can wait. I won't go in with you feeling this unwell."

Beside the sink inside the room is a sick bag. I pass it to Charlotte as we exit the room toward the reception area. The nurse, which previously checked on us, notices us walking toward her.

"You don't look so well, Mrs. Edwards," she cross-examines from across the desk.

"I want my wife checked out immediately. If my surgery needs to be postponed, then so be it."

"You can leave Mrs. Edwards with me, and I'll have her checked out while you still have the surgery?"

I shake my head in disapproval. "No, sorry. I will not leave her in this state. I don't care who I need to speak to, send them my way. My priority is my wife."

The nurse nods with timid eyes. Great, now I've scared her. Thankfully, she scurries away and returns with a doctor a few minutes later.

"Mr. Edwards, I'm Dr. Rooney. If you follow me, I'll examine your wife."

We walk across the corridor to a small examination room. Dr. Rooney is a young doctor, much to my annoyance. Not that I'm one to ever observe someone's looks, but the guy is attractive. *He better not look at Charlotte in a compromising way.*

"Mrs. Edwards, if you can, please lie down on the table and just point out where it hurts."

Charlotte manages to lie on the table as I stand beside her. Dr. Rooney presses his hands softly where Charlotte indicates the pain was felt. With his stethoscope, he listens to her heartbeat. Moments later, he removes it from his ears.

"How long have you been presenting symptoms?"

"Just today," Charlotte answers.

"Have you been exposed to anyone with similar symptoms?" he continues to question. "There are a number of viral infections circulating."

"Uh... no. Our girls have all been well."

He nods, then glances at me. "How many children do you have?"

"Three girls," I answer for Charlotte.

"And you were here for a vasectomy, correct?"

My brows draw in. "Yes, what are you getting at?"

"Have you been using contraceptives?"

Charlotte clears her throat. "Yes, I was on the pill."

"Was?" I blurt out.

"I stopped a week ago because I knew you were getting the snip."

Dr. Rooney waits for us to finish talking.

"Stopping your pill a week ago won't be the reason you're unwell," he informs us, then leans over and retrieves a sample cup from the shelf. "However, there are some things I'd like to rule out, so if you can please use the bathroom and provide me with a urine sample, we can go from there."

My stomach sinks with a heaviness expanding all over my core. Charlotte doesn't say a word, quietly sitting up and walking to the bathroom. She closes the door behind her as I bury my head in my hands.

Please don't be the reason.

Thankfully, Dr. Rooney doesn't talk to me, allowing me a moment to compose myself. Charlotte walks back into the room, avoiding my eyes, passing the sample to Dr. Rooney. He works in silence as we sit here quietly.

"Have there been other health concerns of late?" he asks, but then he glances over, his expression changing with a slight smile forming on his lips.

"No, nothing," Charlotte replies.

"Well, Mrs. Edwards, you're pregnant."

I fucking knew it.

He lifts the pregnancy test, revealing the two positive lines. My face immediately falls, a mixture of shock and disbelief. Charlotte's mouth falls open on the bed before she covers it and rushes back to the bathroom. The sounds echo rather unpleasantly, but I give her time until she emerges minutes later.

"Sorry," she mumbles.

"Nothing to be sorry about," Dr. Rooney assures her. "How about I give you a few minutes to process the news, and I'll return and do a sonogram? We can see how far along you are, then take action from there."

The door closes behind Dr. Rooney, leaving me alone with Charlotte. I'm waiting on her to yell at me, blaming me for making her pregnant. She'll call me selfish and greedy, unable to keep my dick in my pants.

I wait and wait, but it doesn't come.

"I don't know what to say." She wraps her hands around her stomach with her head lowered, unable to look at me.

"Aren't you going to yell at me?"

Charlotte's lips twist in sympathy. "We keep defying the odds. Maybe, though ..."

"Maybe though, what?"

"This is my fault. Do you remember when I had that very stressful foster case? And I had to fly up to Seattle for three days? It was just before we went to Australia."

"Yes... I remember..."

"Well, when packing my bag, Ava took my lipstick, and I got distracted. I went to her room where she was playing dress-ups and, of course, had broken my favorite lipstick. When I went back to the room, I was so annoyed and forgot to pack my pill," she informs me with a remorseful expression.

I tilt my head in confusion. "Weren't you gone for three nights?"

"Yes, but obviously, that's all it took."

My eyes close in frustration as my hands clench into

fists. "Jesus fucking Christ, Charlotte. Why didn't you tell me?"

"I forgot!" she yells in exasperation.

There's a gentle knock on the door before Dr. Rooney walks in. He quickly prepares the machine, followed by spreading the gel across Charlotte's abdomen.

"Now, it may be too early to see anything. Also, your bladder may not be full. However, let's see what we can find."

My eyes focus on the screen, waiting for him to get the right angle. The image on the screen moves, but then I see the small-shaped image the size of a little peanut. Warmth spreads across my chest, just like it has every single time we saw our girls for the first time.

Then, my gaze darts back to the screen, eyes widening as something else catches my attention. Suddenly, my mouth falls open as I continue to stare avidly with my breathing coming to a complete standstill.

"It's twins."

SEVENTEEN

The time when I became a Grandpapa

The phone begins to ring on the desk in the middle of a meeting.

Immediately, my eyes dart to the screen to catch a glimpse of the caller in case it's important. Amelia's name flashes on the screen. I contemplate answering it but decide to leave it for now as everyone waits for the phone to stop ringing. When it does, I assume the call will go to voicemail, and she'll leave a message or send me a text.

Noah continues his presentation on projected numbers for our new hotel chain opening in Singapore until my phone rings again.

"Excuse me. I must take this call."

With my phone in hand, I quickly exit the room into the corridor, closing the door behind me before answering.

"Amelia, is everything okay?"

"Dad, I'm sorry to bother you. I know you're working," she rushes, her tone making me worry. "Is there any chance you and Mom can fly out to Manhattan? There's something important Will and I need to discuss with you."

"Just me and your mother?"

"Actually, Rocky and Nikki will be there as well."

The second their names are mentioned, I know exactly why. My lips press together in a slight grimace as I scratch the back of my neck. I'd come to terms with Amelia being a married woman, but I'd hoped they'd wait to fall pregnant. Amelia is still studying and has only started working more days. There's plenty of time for them to start a family. I don't understand why the rush.

I choose not to voice my suspicions. Instead, pretend I have no clue what's going on.

"We'll fly out tonight and see you in the morning."

"Thanks, Dad." She breathes a sigh of relief. "You know I love you, right?"

"Yes, sweetheart. And I love you too."

We hang up the call at the same time my chest tightens beneath the suit I wear. Before heading back in, I quickly dial Charlotte's number.

"Hey," she answers. "I know why you're calling me, but I'm walking into a client's office."

"We're leaving tonight. Addison can watch Alexa. I expect we'll be gone no more than a few days. Adriana can check on the girls."

"Just breathe, Lex," Charlotte assures me. "It'll be okay."

"She's too young."

"Amelia is married now. She's no longer your little girl."

My shoulders fall as a heavy sigh escapes me. "Charlotte, she'll always be my little girl."

"I'm hoping we're here because you've got exciting news to tell us?" Rocky gazes at me with an animated smile. "My son isn't shooting blanks."

Jesus fucking Christ. This man cannot be tamed.

Amelia glances at Will as something passes between them. Their expression is much more serious than expected, which starts to worry me someone is sick. After what happened with Elijah, I'm on edge whenever someone calls a family meeting to discuss something important.

"Yes, but it's not quite what you think..." Amelia fore-warns everyone. "Will and I have made the decision to adopt Ashley's baby."

Silence falls over the room before Will takes over. "I know what you're all thinking. We just got married. Both Amelia and I feel very strongly about wanting to adopt the baby. It doesn't sit right with either of us that he will be placed in the foster system like many other children. So, we're hoping with the two best attorneys helping us, we can make him a part of our family."

The first person to react is Charlotte, of course. She reaches her hand out to place it on top of Amelia's. Squeezing her hand reassuringly, a smile spreads across Amelia's lips as her shoulders relax.

"Mom, you'll help us?" Amelia asks.

"Of course, honey," Charlotte answers with a choke in her voice. "I've always felt strongly about adoption. Your father and I talked about it often, but life had other plans, and the four of you came along. It wasn't in the cards for us, but it doesn't mean it isn't for you. This baby will be so loved and deserves a family after all he's gone through in such a short amount of time."

I'm still trying to process the news. Adoption, while positively impacting parents and children's lives, can also have its downfalls. What if the adoption process fails? What if the biological father wants custody later in life? Stewart Knight comes from a lineage of blue blood. It can get ugly if his family finds out he has a son.

My muscles tense, but I refuse to show my emotions, not wanting to start an argument and this ending badly.

Unlike Charlotte, Nikki sits back in her chair with a concerned face. "This is very short notice."

Will glances at his mother with an annoyed expression. "Yeah, life has a way of throwing things your way when you least expect it. So, what answer will satisfy you?"

"Will," Rocky scolds in a deep, cemented tone. "Mom's just trying to help you."

Nikki crosses her arms, unwelcoming with her stern gaze. Obviously, she's not pleased with their decision, so chances are this will blow up any minute now.

"If you want to help us, why are we wasting time questioning the adoption? For every minute which passes, he's alone in that hospital with two grandparents who can barely manage to take care of themselves," Will fires off, unable to control his temper.

Will stands from the table, leaving the room to compose himself. Amelia rises, but I motion for her to sit down. I've spent a lot of time with Will, and when he's passionate about something, he's all in.

"I'll talk to him."

Inside the kitchen, Will is standing with his hands resting on the countertop. His shoulders appear tense, and every breath he takes is almost a growl.

"Why is my mother a pain in the ass?"

A soft chuckle leaves me as I try to lighten the mood. "That's one way to describe her. I remember how protective she was when I ran into Charlotte in Manhattan. The thorn in my side."

Will rubs his face vigorously. Unlike the usually confident man I'm used to seeing in the boardroom, he looks defeated.

"So, who brought up the idea of the adoption?"

"Amelia," he resigns. "She had been acting distant, very unsettled. One night, I kind of got fed up and asked her to talk because I'm not a mind reader. She told me what she was feeling. I mean, I was shocked. We hadn't really spoken about starting our own family."

"Sounds just like her mother."

"The more she opened up, the more I began to feel the same way. Something drew us to this little boy, and how can I let him grow up in a foster system?" Will asks with a choke in his voice. "All this money means nothing if I can't help save someone's life."

"Look, I know you're capable of many things, but raising a child isn't easy," I tell him firmly. "There's a lot of sacrifices to be made."

"I know," he mumbles, then fixates his gaze on me. "Which is why we've decided to move to the West Coast. Amelia wants to be close to Charlotte, and you, of course."

I try to hold back my feelings, but if the truth be told, having our daughter close to us and seeing her often makes me happy. I know Charlotte will feel the exact same, and given there's a potential grandchild joining us, even more so. If only Ava would consider moving back, but that girl is headstrong and living her best life, according to her.

"Have you told your parents?"

Will shakes his head. "And I guess they won't take it well, but I can deal with them. What I need help with is setting up in LA with an office space. Everything is running so smoothly here, plus going through all this adoption stuff, it's just a lot to handle."

I place my hand on his shoulder to reassure him. "You leave that stuff to me, Noah, and Kate."

"Thanks, Dad." Will mocks with a grin.

We walk back into the room as everyone's eyes turn to us.

"Done with your tantrum now?" Rocky snickers.

Will rolls his eyes at his father, then takes a seat as Amelia grabs his hand to bring it to her lips. It dawns on me at this moment there's nothing to worry about. Will and Amelia have gone through a lot, all of which have strengthened their bond. If anyone is going to be great adoptive parents, it's these two.

"So, do we have your help?" Will directs his stare toward Nikki.

Nikki's expression softens. "You always had my help. I'm just protective, okay?"

Rocky snorts. "Control freak."

"There's just one more thing," Amelia mentions cautiously. "We've decided to move to LA. I know it means I have to leave the firm, but it's important for us to have space and a bigger home should our family expand in the future."

"We raised a kid in the city. Two, actually," Rocky reminds us.

"I know." Amelia nods as her eyes glaze over while gazing at Charlotte. "But, well, I kinda need Mom around. Being a mother is terrifying, and well..."

Nikki places her hand on Amelia's. "Relax, I get it. I'm not offended, but I will miss you guys."

"I'm offended," Rocky blurts out, crossing his arms. "I'm close to retiring and could have babysat full-time."

"How are you close to retiring?" Nikki argues, leaning back to interrogate him. "Your job is to commentate, then hang out at after parties drinking beer with athletes and groupies. Quote, you said you get paid to live your best life and relished at being called a DILF. To add, you're barely home, and when you do come home, you're drunk as fuck. You took your pants off and started dry humping the refrigerator."

"One time, don't you forget anything?" Rocky drags but then cocks his head to the side with a smirk. "Were you complaining when you were on all fours getting the best—"

"We're done," Will raises his voice in annoyance. "Mom, Charlie, let's get right to work. We have a son we need to bring home."

"We're home."

The door opens as Will and Amelia walk through into the foyer of their new house. Charlotte follows behind them, having accompanied them on their trip back from Florida. Amelia begged Charlotte to come, worried she might drop the baby or do something stupid.

The last few months had been a whirlwind. I was busy with Noah and Kate, making sure Will was set up in LA and ready to go. It wasn't just securing a building and fitting everything out. It was hiring new staff and organizing for existing staff to move to the West Coast. If anything, Will's executive team is loyal. Not one of them had an issue with transferring at such short notice.

Ava and Eric took care of setting up the house along with Adriana, who organized all the baby items. Charlotte and Nikki were occupied, ensuring all the legal documents were filed correctly to make this possible.

The moment my eyes set upon Amelia, she appeared different. There's a glow on her face and a happiness words cannot describe. Will, too, looks relieved to be home.

"Oh my god, he's here!" Adriana claps her hands with excitement. "I can't wait to have grandkids."

Luna and Willow snort beside her. "Calm down, Mom. You're going to be waiting a while."

Adriana waves her hand in dismissal. "I'll be forever waiting on you two. But I've got Andy..."

Julian lets out a huff while rolling his eyes. "Leave him alone. He's living life on his terms without you butting in."

I must give it to him, he's not afraid to put my sister in her place, and I agree about Andy. It's his life, and Adriana shouldn't push him to settle down.

Will places the carrier firmly on the ground. With ease, he gently removes the baby and cradles him in his arms. He looks like a natural, in his element as a father.

The baby is passed around as I observe each one of our family members meeting our newest addition.

"Do we have a name?" Addison asks, rocking her nephew.

"Ashton Alexander Edwards Romano," Amelia says proudly, then raises her eyes to meet mine. "Dad, are you ready?"

I don't know if I'll ever be ready, but then Amelia takes baby Ashton from Addison and carefully places him in my arms.

Unconditional love is a funny thing. When it settles within you, there's no turning back. It becomes a part of who you are.

And just like that, the hole inside my heart from losing my own son becomes a little bit smaller.

All because of the little boy resting in my arms.

My grandson.

EIGHTEEN

Present

"How was London?"

Will continues our small talk as we sit in my office signing a contract. Another day, another business deal. Nothing unusual when you're an entrepreneur running billion-dollar investments.

"It gave me a lot to think about."

Will signs his name and then places the pen down, leaning back into the chair.

"Let me take a wild guess," he says while rubbing his chin. "About how easily your life could have taken a different path?"

I glance up at him. "How did you know?"

"There's something about London," he begins, then stalls, keeping his thoughts to himself for a moment like this is something he's thought about often. "It's the place to escape your troubles, but the darkness never leaves."

"It was a long time ago," I mutter.

"Right, and you have a beautiful wife, daughters, and a million grandchildren now," he muses.

"About that," I say with a knowing grin. "When are you going to get the snip? I don't know how many more grandkids I can take."

Will chuckles. "When did you?"

"I tried, but Alexa surprised us."

"You tried?" he repeats in a mocking tone. "Sounds to me like you chickened out. Afraid it would damage the goods."

I sign the final dotted line and then place my pen down. "Sometimes, my friend, life has a way of working itself out."

"What you meant to say is Charlie took it for the team?"

"Perhaps," I respond with a smirk. "We're all done here. Time to start our next project."

When it comes to business, Will understands the importance of being ahead of the game. We may have just signed off on something big, but it doesn't end here. Despite Charlotte telling me to slow down, I'll be the first to admit it's one of the hardest things to do.

"Let's go have dinner before Charlotte finds me working during what is supposed to be family time."

We leave my office and head outside to the patio. It's a warm night with the sun still out. Charlotte and Ava set the table while Austin took care of the grill.

Masen is chasing the kids around the big backyard. Even though his brother was the athletic one in the family, Masen's stamina outdid the kids. I'm quite surprised, given the boys have so much energy.

Amelia is standing behind Emmy, braiding her hair while ensuring her kids stay out of trouble simultaneously.

"I can't believe Masen outran Ashton and Archer.

Those boys are fast," Amelia comments, shaking her head in disbelief.

"When you're done with her hair, can you do mine?" Addison begs. "Fishtail, please."

Amelia glances at Alexa, who, no surprise, is on her phone. "And what about you? Do you want your hair done too, like I have nothing better to do?"

Alexa keeps her eyes lowered, then mumbles. "No, thanks."

Since our return from London and Alexa's outburst, I still haven't mentioned to Charlotte what Alexa said to me. As for our encounters, there haven't been any. Alexa has ignored me at all costs, and I'm assuming tonight will be no different.

"What crawled up your ass and died?" Ava butts in, carrying a plate of food. "You got your rags?"

Addison shakes her head. "No one calls it that."

"Shark week," Ava adds, much to my disgust.

"That's disgusting," Amelia expresses while cringing. "The only perk to being pregnant is not having your periods for like a year."

"Here, here," Ava brags. "So, what's wrong?"

"Nothing's wrong," Alexa states, still avoiding everyone.

The older three look at each other, but something passes between them. I expect they'll ambush Alexa again any minute, but Charlotte announces dinner is ready, prompting everyone to take a seat.

We all take a spot at the table, then Ashton announces he wants to say grace. His small but confident voice is heard all around us, bringing our family together.

As I look around, I'm overwhelmed by the emotion of feeling incredibly blessed. I reach out to touch Charlotte's hand as she glances at me with a loving gaze. We may have done many things wrong, but those mistakes led us here.

"So, Masen and I have set a date for the wedding," Addison announces with excitement. "It's nine months from now, and if Mom and Dad are okay with it, we'd love to have the ceremony at our chateau in France."

"Of course, honey," Charlotte assures her. "It's beautiful in spring—"

"Hold on," Ava interrupts. "Nine months because..."

"Because it's the only time we can get a whole six weeks off," Addison quickly interjects.

"There's no baby." Masen glares at Ava, setting the record straight. "Work is hectic. We've just acquired another publishing house. It's hard enough taking care of the damn bearded dragon Addison insisted we buy."

"Hey, don't talk bad about Mr. Hemsworth. He's been nothing but good to you," Addison chastises.

Amelia begins to laugh. "You ended up calling him that?"

"Bearded dragons are native to Australia. It was only fitting his name represented an Aussie."

"A handsome Aussie," Ava quips.

"Okay, stop now before this conversation falls into the Hemsworth brother's rabbit hole again," Will complains.

I take a sip of the wine Charlotte poured, then clear my throat. "The chateau will be perfect. I'll make sure my schedule is clear."

The girls begin to talk about wedding plans which, frankly, bores me. I engage in conversation with Austin as he talks about what's happening with work. Even though I chose not to follow a career in medicine, I live vicariously through his stories. A part of me wishes one of the girls studied to be a doctor, but all of them freaked out when it came to anything medical. For the better part, Addison is the closest to the medical field.

Our conversation is short-lived as the kids grow bored and begin interrupting all the adults. Charlotte manages to get them to behave with the promise of dessert.

After dessert is served, it's obvious the kids are heading downhill. Will and Amelia are the first to leave, then Austin and Ava. Masen and Addison stick around for a bit but then head over to Haden and Presley's for a nightcap.

I welcome the silence when everyone is gone, taking a deep breath and enjoying the summer's night. That is until I notice Alexa sitting alone at the table. It's unusual, given she's the first to disappear to her bedroom. While cleaning up the table, Charlotte glances at me with curiosity but then places the plates down.

"Is everything okay, honey?"

Alexa's hands spread out on the table, unable to look at either one of us. She lets out a small breath while straightening her shoulders with a strong stance.

"Can you both sit down for a moment? There's something I want to tell you."

I take a seat beside Charlotte, knowing whatever I'm about to hear will not be music to my ears. If she's been unable to talk to me for this long, it's highly unlikely she's going to say something pleasant.

"I've decided not to go to college."

The bile rises in my throat, the same time my chest tightens. I try to control my emotions, remembering Charlotte's wise words, but anger is a beast that can't always be tamed.

"Alexa," Charlotte stammers, "I... I don't understand where this is coming from?"

"This is coming from someone who doesn't want to go

to college," she responds coldly. "Just because my sisters went doesn't mean I have to."

Charlotte stares in confusion. "So, what exactly will you be doing?"

"I'll be traveling around Europe."

"Then, when you're done, say, in a year? You're going to enroll?" Charlotte pushes.

In slow motion, Alexa's bitter eyes lock into mine. "No."

Her stare weighs heavily, and it's more than teenage angst. *What the hell have I done to raise such an ungrateful child?* Alexa's head tilts away, unable to look at me any longer. The contempt she has for me leaves me speechless, but of course, the anger swirling within me refuses to subside.

The skin around my eyes tightens as my jaw sets.

"You have one year to travel," I state in an arctic tone, strangling my voice to control my temper. "Then, you will return and enrol in college."

Alexa stands up in a rush, crossing her arms with a defiant stare. "You don't get a say in my life anymore. I'm almost eighteen."

"As long as you live under this roof..."

"Well, guess what, *Lex...*" she drags my name in a condescending tone. "As soon as I graduate, I will no longer be living under this roof. You can control what you want, but you will never control me."

And as quickly as she drops this bombshell on us, Alexa runs into the house and out of sight.

I bury my head into my hands, unable to shake the animosity from what just happened. In the blink of an eye, I'm sitting here counting my blessings to being disrespected by my own daughter.

I thought I'd experienced the worse when I found out

Will and Amelia were lying to me and sneaking behind my back. The anger toward them was unparalleled. I'd never experienced such contempt as I had when I discovered the man I'd mentored was ultimately fucking my daughter.

As for Ava, her pregnancy with Austin was a surprise and at the time, a disappointment. Yet, I soon learned how mistakes equate to blessings. Many said I became soft and treated Ava differently, but I argued the circumstances were entirely different.

Addison has never put me in a position ever to get mad at her. So, perhaps, I thought the worse was over.

But rainbows don't form until after the storm.

The storm known as Alexandra Adriana Edwards has just made landfall.

And she's ready to *destroy* everything in sight....

To be continued in Craving Love...

"I'm guessing Daddy didn't see you leaving the house like this?"

Cole grabs my hand as we enter the crowded house for Mikayla's eighteenth birthday party. Considering it's a school night, everyone from senior year is here. Apparently, the reason behind the Thursday night party is because Mikayla's parents are taking her to Europe tomorrow. If only we all had such relaxed parents.

"He didn't see me," I say over the loud music. "I left before he came home."

Cole leans in, brushing his lips against my ear. *"You look fucking hot."*

I force a fake smile as we walk into the large living room, pretending the compliment makes me happy. Cole looks handsome tonight, dressed in a white tee with a gold chain around his neck. His white sneakers are brand new, standing out against his dark denim jeans.

He runs his hand through his black hair, nodding to greet people but then stops and says hello to his friends. Most of them are from the football team, jocks just like him.

Hanging out with the boys can get tedious since all they talk about is chicks they want to screw. Half the girls wouldn't touch these guys for the life of them. The newest challenge they set upon themselves is trying to take the virginity of some new girl. All I know is that she's quiet and keeps to herself. She does come across as nerdy with her thick black glasses and weird obsession with wearing plaid, but nevertheless, his friends have no chance.

Five minutes into hanging around the guys, and I'm already bored. I excuse myself to walk around, saying hello to a few friends before making my way outside to the pool. I'm surprised by how many people are in the water and not so surprised when I see a guy throwing up on the side.

It's a warm enough night to swim. I'm not exactly dressed for it, already pushing my limits with the dress I wear. It dawned on me a pair of jeans would have been much more comfortable, but I wanted to prove a point to myself.

Life can go back to normal.

I can move on.

Near the outdoor grill is a table with drinks. It's obvious the punch is spiked, which is why it's popular, and people keep helping themselves. I contemplate having a drink, but my mood doesn't call for it.

A set of arms wrap around my waist as the familiar cologne lingers in the air. My chest rises, then falls, remembering all the good times we have had over the last year since we started dating.

"Let's go upstairs," Cole suggests with a flirtatious tone. "I want you alone."

There is only so much I can say to distract him, but I try anyway.

"There are a lot of people. I'm sure the rooms are occupied."

He leans in to whisper, "There's a secret room no one knows about."

My eyes wander to the pink-colored punch floating in the large bowl. With a deep breath, I pour myself a cup and drink it in one go. A rasp escapes me, the alcohol content stronger than anticipated.

Cole laughs, then does the same. Unlike me, he holds his drinks much better. There was only one time when I pushed the limits, and it didn't end well. Thank God Ava rescued me, or I would have been grounded for life.

Without another word, Cole grabs my hand and leads me to a flight of stairs near the kitchen. The house is big, though not as big as mine, and I have no clue where he is taking me.

Down the long hallway, there are several doors, but Cole opens the one all the way at the end. The room itself appears to be a guest room. Its furnishings are minimal, with a king-size bed being the focus of the room.

Cole closes the door behind me, leading us to the bed. He doesn't waste any time, pressing his lips against mine forcefully. His hands wander beneath my dress, causing me to tense. *Just get it over and done with, I beg of myself.*

"What's wrong?" Cole pulls back. "Why don't you want me to fuck you?"

Another moment where I can tell him the truth, just like all the other moments which presented themselves. But what's the point? It's over, and everything should go back to normal.

"I've got a lot on my mind," I half tell the truth.

"Someone else is on your mind?"

"Cole, there's no one else. It's only been you."

Unlike many girls in senior year, I've only been with one guy. After months of begging, I finally gave in one night. It wasn't an ideal situation since it happened at another party and finished quickly when the door opened, and Cole's best friend caught us.

"Yeah, well, you're making me feel like shit," he complains.

I pull back, resting on my elbows. "Just because I don't feel like fucking you?"

Cole jumps off the bed, pacing with his hands running through his hair. His blue eyes watch me, almost as if I'm doing something wrong by not giving in to him tonight. *He doesn't understand. He'll never understand.*

Suddenly, a piercing scream startles us both. It came from outside, so I run to the window to see what is happening. My eyes widen in shock as a body is dragged from the pool, unconscious.

Without a second thought, I bolt out of the room, leaving Cole behind as adrenaline runs through my veins. The fresh air hits my face when I make it outside, but I rush to the scene.

"Someone call 9-1-1!"

People gather around the boy lying unconscious by the side of the pool. They uselessly stare in bewilderment, but no one does a damn thing. I push people aside, then fall to my knees to better examine him.

I'd watched a YouTube video on how to perform CPR. One of those nights, I fell down a rabbit hole leading me to medical videos. I was fascinated with it all, unsure why but hoping it sticks.

Remembering each step, I attempt to perform CPR. Thankfully, he has a pulse, but how long will all depend on what I do next.

I hear the voice in my head repeating the steps. As people watch on, I begin with the chest compressions using my body weight and keeping my arms straight, then press straight down. Next, I release the pressure before giving mouth-to-mouth.

"Alexa, what the fuck are you doing?" Cole questions angrily. "Paramedics will be here any minute."

Another minute and we might lose him.

Don't let this happen.

I place one hand on his forehead and the other under his chin to tilt the head back so his airways open. Pinching the soft part of his nose so it closes, I open his mouth with my thumb and fingers.

As I take a breath, Cole continues to yell at me, but I ignore him, placing my lips over the guy's mouth and then begin blowing steadily. When I pull back, a rough cough escapes his lips before he shuffles to his side and starts expelling water.

"Alexa," Mikayla screams, pressing on my shoulders. "You saved him!"

Still on my knees, I sit back and watch as the guy opens his eyes, disoriented. The paramedics arrive, running through the crowd with their equipment. The noise fades out, all the scene becoming a sudden blur.

"You saved his life," the paramedic praises as they continue to examine him. "Ever considered a career in medicine?"

Cole deliberately raises his brows while cocking his head. "Dr. Edwards, just like Daddy."

The memories come flashing back, the times I'd begged my older sisters to play hospital with me after I'd stolen Dad's stethoscope from his office drawer.

But I'd rather die than fall hostage to my father's hopes and dreams for me.

"I'm glad he's alive," I mutter beneath my breath. "I want to go home."

Cole crosses his arms in defiance. "Well, I want to stay."

I turn my back on him and ignore everyone as I make my way outside. Reaching for my purse, I open the Uber app, but it shows no one available. Just fucking great.

Scrolling through my phone, I realize all my sisters flew out tonight. There's no chance in hell I'm calling my parents since I'm already in trouble given all Mom's messages. I dial my cousin Luna's number, and thankfully she picks up.

Twenty minutes later, we're on the way home.

"Does Uncle Lex know you're out this late on a school night?" Luna asks, pulling into my street.

"I'll deal with it tomorrow."

"Aren't you afraid of being grounded?"

I shrug. "Not really."

As we pull into the driveway, Luna leaves the car running. "You sure you don't want to talk about it?"

"I'm fine, thanks again."

With my purse in hand, I exit the car and take a deep breath. If all goes well, I can run up to my room so I'm not caught in this short yellow dress I borrowed from Ava.

The second I step inside, I turn the light on to see my father. His presence in the darkness catches me by surprise, and his eyes turn angry upon noticing my dress.

"Oh," I mouth, avoiding eye contact.

"Oh?" he repeats in a cold tone. "Is that the only response I'll get from you, considering it's two hours past your curfew, and it's a school night?"

Growing up as the youngest daughter of a well-known billionaire is not glamorous like everything thinks it is.

My father, Lex Edwards, controls everything our family does. My sisters may have moved out, but I'm the last one under his wrath.

God forbid I do anything to disobey him. He demands respect, but I'm so over his controlling ways. I continue to ignore him, flicking my long hair over my shoulder in complete disregard for his authority.

"Anything you'd like to say, Alexandra?"

A puff of air leaves my lips as I roll my eyes in annoyance.

"Let me guess. You're calling me Alexandra, so I'm in big trouble? Assuming I'm grounded, you'll take all my privileges off me because you are the controlling Lex Edwards."

His eyes widen as his nostrils flare. Lowering his gaze for a moment, he's obviously trying to control himself because Mom told him to.

"You're damn right you're grounded," he shouts, slamming his fist on the counter. "How dare you worry your mother and me over your careless actions. You live in this house. You abide by our rules."

Of course, he has no sympathy. He has no idea what happened tonight, and even if I told him the truth, he'd find a way to turn it into all about his rules.

"I'm over your rules!" I yell back, eyes blazing with fire. "I didn't ask to be Lex Edwards daughter. This life was thrust upon me."

"This life?" He tilts his head in confusion. "A life of having a roof over your head, food on the table, private schooling? I'm sorry. Please explain how awful it is for you to have what many children have to fight for."

If only he knew the truth.

I drop my eyes to the floor. "You have no idea."

"No idea how spoiled you are? You have everything you want. Please, enlighten me. How terrible it is to grow up as our daughter?"

Slowly, I lift my gaze to meet his matching emerald eyes. He waits for me to respond, but what is there to say?

"I hate you."

And as quick as the words leave my mouth, I exit the kitchen and run up to my bedroom. Shutting the door behind me, I lean back against it as tears fall down my cheeks.

It's all his fault.

I aborted Cole's baby because of him.

And now, I must live with this decision for the rest of my life.

All because I carry the Edwards' name ...

ALSO BY KAT T. MASEN

The Dark Love Series

Featuring Lex & Charlie

Chasing Love: A Billionaire Love Triangle

Chasing Us: A Second Chance Love Triangle

Chasing Her: A Stalker Romance

Chasing Him: A Forbidden Second Chance Romance

Chasing Fate: An Enemies-to-Lovers Romance

Chasing Heartbreak: A Friends-to-Lovers Romance

The Forbidden Love Series

(Dark Love Series Second Generation)

Featuring Amelia Edwards

The Trouble With Love: An Age Gap Romance

The Trouble With Us: A Second Chance Love Triangle

The Trouble With Him: A Secret Pregnancy Romance

The Trouble With Her: A Friends-to-Lovers Romance

The Trouble With Fate: An Enemies-to-Lovers Romance

Also by Kat T. Masen

The Office Rival: An Enemies-to-Lovers Romance

The Marriage Rival: An Office Romance

Bad Boy Player: A Brother's Best Friend Romance

Roomie Wars Box Set (Books 1 to 3): Friends-to-Lovers Series

ABOUT THE AUTHOR

Born and bred in Sydney, Australia, **Kat T. Masen** is a mother to four crazy boys and wife to one sane husband. Growing up in a generation where social media and fancy gadgets didn't exist, she enjoyed reading from an early age and found herself immersed in these stories. After meeting friends on Twitter who loved to read as much as she did, her passion for writing began, and the friendships continued on despite the distance.

"I'm known to be crazy and humorous. Show me the most random picture of a dog in a wig, and I'll be laughing for days."

Download free bonus content, purchase signed paperbacks & bookish merchandise.

Visit: **www.kattmasen.com**

CPSIA information can be obtained
at www.ICGtesting.com
Printed in the USA
LVHW041650060523
746309LV00003B/325